FOLLOW THE LEADER

FOLLOW THE LEADER

FRANCINE GARSON

Follow the Leader

By Francine Garson

Copyright © 2019 by Francine Garson

Cover design by Cherie Foxley

~

We dance round in a ring and suppose, but the Secret sits in
the middle and knows.
–Robert Frost, *The Secret Sits*

The best way of keeping a secret is to pretend there isn't one.
–Margaret Atwood, *The Blind Assassin*

PART I

1

---

race opened the mailbox and pulled out the usual—advertising circulars, requests for donations, statements, bills—and a large manila envelope, her name and address written across it in a familiar loopy script. An icy chill ran up her spine as she eyed the sender's name.

Paula Milgram, the dot of the *i* in her last name replaced with a tiny heart.

Shaking her head, Grace pulled her lower lip into her mouth and with the pile of mail pressed to her chest, hurried up the driveway and into the house. Without bothering to take her jacket off, she dumped everything onto the kitchen table and ripped open the manila envelope.

A folded sheet of paper and a cascade of pictures spilled out. She flipped through black and white Polaroids of herself and Paula smiling behind a makeshift lemonade stand, hugging matching teddy bears in Paula's bedroom, and grinning in front of a carrot-nosed snowman in her own backyard. She glanced at faded color shots of the two of them sitting side by side at a picnic table and posing in long pastel dresses with their prom dates.

Then, the San Francisco pictures. Grace combed through them, her breathing shallow and her heartbeat fast. But...nothing. Just the typical shots of buildings, streets, and overhyped landmarks. *Whew!* She sighed in relief, a long stream of air gushing out of her mouth. Sliding a chair away from the table, she lowered herself into it.

But why now? After so many years, why now?

She reached for the sheet of paper, unfolded it, and began to read.

Hi Gracie,

I know we haven't been in touch for a while. So you're probably surprised to hear from me. Hope you're happy though. I've moved around a lot, but I've been in North Carolina for the past couple of years. Anyway, I'll be heading up to Brooklyn in a couple of weeks for my brother, Joey's (remember him?) daughter's wedding. I'm taking the train, and I'll be stopping in New York City before I go to his house. I would have called you, but I don't know your number, and I didn't want to just call you out of the blue anyway. I don't know your email address either. But I do want to see you. So call me, okay?

Love,
Paula
(555) 555-IIII

Paula...

Was it the place, or was it the time? Or was it some kind of serendipitous combination of forces that just happened to explode in *that* particular place at *that* particular time?

San Francisco, 1967. They called it the Summer of Love, but that was only part of it. It was the summer that changed everything. Or maybe it was just the summer that everything changed. Something ended, and something else began.

Even now, more than fifty years later, Grace wasn't quite sure what happened. Or why. She only knew that she had made a mistake that summer. A big one. Paula had too. And Grace was lucky that neither she, nor anyone in her family, had had to suffer the consequences of her carelessness, her stupidity. Yes, Grace, Dawn, and Joanna...they were all very, very lucky.

So was Paula.

Some things were better left in the past. Buried under the years of time.

Hopefully, Paula knew that too.

2

Peering between the slats of the dining room blinds, Joanna watched for Grace-ma's Volkswagen Beetle. *Grace-ma*, the name Joanna, as a two-year-old, had invented for her grandmother. And to Joanna, her grandmother had always been Grace-ma. *Her* Grace-ma.

She spotted the car turning into the cul-de-sac and grabbed her denim jacket. Slinging her bag over her shoulder, she dashed out the door.

The convertible top was down, and Grace-ma's silver-streaked blonde braid trailed down the back of her striped poncho. Her mouth burst into a wide smile when Joanna slid into the seat next to her, and she leaned over and pulled her granddaughter into a warm hug.

"Grace-ma!" Joanna kissed her grandmother's cheek.

"My darling girl," Grace-ma said, running her hand through Joanna's hair. "Do you have a clip?"

"Do I have a clip? What kind of question is that?" Joanna laughed and pulled a leather stick barrette out of her bag. She scooped her hair into a ponytail, twisted it up, and folded it over. Positioning the hand-tooled leather rectangle against her head, she slid the stick through it.

Very retro. Very Grace-ma.

Grace-ma nodded her approval, and they were off. The wind was a gentle tickle on Joanna's face and a soft rustle through her hair, lifting the strands that escaped from her barrette. The radio was tuned to a classic rock station, and Crosby, Stills, and Nash sang their ode to "wooden ships on the water."

Joanna sang the harmony. "Talkin' 'bout very free and easy…"

Grace-ma drove and smiled.

Her house was just a ten-minute drive away, but it might as well have been in a different time zone. Joanna knew her grandmother could have afforded a luxury apartment somewhere or one of the newly built McMansions, designed to look old, like the one she lived in with her own parents. Instead, Grace-ma still lived in the house she and Grandpa Doug had bought in the 1970s, the house where Joanna's mom had grown up. Joanna's parents had tried to convince her to look for something smaller and newer, but she wouldn't do it. She said she knew what was best for her.

And she was right, Joanna thought. She did know.

Grace-ma parked the car at the top of the driveway. Arm in arm, she and Joanna walked up the stone path and climbed the four wooden steps leading to the wraparound porch that was just one of her reasons for refusing to move. She fit the key into the lock and pushed the door open.

Just inside, Hendrix, Grace-ma's orange striped cat, sat on his woven mat like a feline Buddha. Stretching out his front legs and curving his back into a U, he yawned and padded over, greeting them with a tail swish that tickled their legs.

Grace-ma slipped her poncho over her head and took Joanna's jacket, adding both to the collection of embroidered shawls, knitted hats, and patterned scarves suspended from the coat rack in the corner.

Joanna picked up Hendrix, cradling his soft warmth, and followed Grace-ma into the kitchen. The green smell of living plants sparked with dashes of sandalwood, chocolate, and sweet vanilla made her smile. Hendrix wiggled out of her arms and raced to the far wall, leaping onto the ledge of its bay window.

Joanna scanned the room, taking in the familiar glass-fronted cabinets stocked with brightly colored Mexican pottery, the long wooden table with its rush back chairs, and the set of wind chimes suspended over the patio door. A trio of plant-filled macramé hangers hung over Hendrix's window seat.

"Cookies?" Grace-ma pointed to the daisy-shaped plate sitting on the tiled counter.

"You have to ask?" Joanna laughed.

Perched on high stools, they sat side by side at the kitchen's center island, dunking their cookies in milk, both knowing it was the best way to eat chocolate chip cookies, or any cookies really, especially when they were homemade. And in Grace-ma's house, cookies were *always* homemade. Between bites, the two chatted in typical grandmother-granddaughter style.

No, Joanna still didn't find school all that difficult. Honors classes, all A's, the usual.

Friends? Well yeah, the usual there too.

Boys? Nah, no one special.

Joanna had always been Grace-ma's good little granddaughter, and she wanted to stay that way. She loved her grandmother. She adored her. So, she told her the things that would make her happy. She told her grandmother the truth. Mostly.

Joanna carried their empty plates and glasses to the sink. "But enough about me. There's really nothing interesting going on." She squirted soap onto the sponge and turned to look over her shoulder. "Do you want to work on the scrapbook?"

Grace draped an old sheet across the long kitchen table and brought out a box of supplies. Joanna lifted its lid, and they both looked down at the jumble of scrapbooking papers, embellishments, squares of fabric, scissors, adhesives, colored pens and pencils, pages ripped from magazines, and rubber banded stacks of photos labeled with yellow sticky notes.

"Think we have everything?" Grace put her hands on her hips and grinned. "Or do we need to make another trip to the arts and crafts shop?"

"I think we're okay for now." Joanna laughed and began to pull the supplies out of the box, laying them in organized groups across the table and leaving a clear area in the center.

Grace carefully slid the scrapbook down from the top shelf of the hall closet and placed it on the table in the open center spot. Joanna ran her hand down the smooth cover of the book. With a finger, she traced the letters of her grandmother's name spelled out in decoupage letters across it.

Grace Crawford Raymond.

"Can we do it together?" Joanna had asked when she had given the scrapbook to her grandmother for her birthday two months earlier.

Grace didn't remember exactly what she had said, but she did remember how she felt, her heart growing bigger and lighter all at once. And so, that beautiful book became a gift that Joanna and Grace were giving to each other, a journey they were taking back in time, digging through the stories of Grace's life.

But Grace needed to be careful, watchful, ever vigilant. Because there were some stories that weren't meant to be told. Not to her granddaughter, not to her daughter, not to anyone. Her mind, unbidden, jumped to the final words of Paula's handwritten note.

But I do want to see you. So call me, okay?

Grace knew she had to respond, and she would…later. But right now, she was going to focus on her granddaughter and the project they were creating together.

Joanna, her dark brown hair a smooth and shiny curtain across her back, leaned over the book. Slowly leafing through the completed pages, she announced each phase of her grandmother's life.

"Childhood, elementary school, high school." Then she looked up, her mouth widening into a grin. "Grace-ma, we're up to 1967." She clapped her hands together. "The Summer of Love."

Grace nodded. "Yes, I suppose we are."

Joanna reached across the table and scooped a mound of rubber banded piles of pictures into a single colorful heap. Tossing aside the stacks of photos documenting her grandparents' wedding, her mother's childhood and her own, and all the events in between, she pulled out the thick pile marked *San Francisco-1967*.

"You took a lot of pictures in San Francisco, Grace-ma," she said, thumbing the edge of the stack.

"I guess I did," Grace said. "Before I left, I used some of

my babysitting money to buy my own Instamatic camera. It was easy to load and light to carry. I took it everywhere that summer."

"Like an old school cell phone, but without the phone?"

Grace chuckled. "That's a good analogy, Joanna," she said, patting her granddaughter's arm.

"Thanks." Joanna smiled.

Picture by picture, Joanna laid out the story of the most important summer of her grandmother's life in straight rows across the table. She pointed to a photo of a teenage Grace in a neatly pressed polka-dotted dress, her blonde hair grazing her shoulders and her growing-out bangs tucked behind her ears. Her curled fingers gripped a plaid suitcase.

"Is this when you first arrived?"

Grace nodded and closed her eyes, tapping her cheek with a finger. Remembering...

Anyway, her granddaughter knew the story—most of it.

Just after graduating from high school, Grace had gone to visit her friend, Paula, who had moved with her family to San Francisco the summer before. The girls had been best friends ever since the fifth grade when Paula had swapped her bologna and cheese sandwich for Grace's peanut butter and jelly while the lunchroom monitor wasn't looking.

Paula's father's transfer to San Francisco had been devastating to both of them. They'd cried, bought each other matching gold ball earrings, and pinky swore to be best friends forever and a day. Long distance phone calls were expensive, so they spoke only as often as their parents allowed. Their weekly letters to each other were so long they usually required extra postage. Then, in a surprise and generous gesture, Grace's parents bought her a round-trip ticket to San Francisco as a high school graduation gift.

Grace opened her eyes and stood up. Leaning over the

table, she scanned the collection of photos, stopping at a shot of herself posed in front of an airport baggage carousel. Her former go-to traveling attire had been exchanged for an outfit of patched bell-bottom jeans and an embroidered peasant shirt, her gold ball earrings replaced with a pair of large silvery hoops. The plaid suitcase looked like it belonged to someone else.

"And this," she said, "was taken on the day I arrived back home in New Jersey."

"You don't even look like the same person, Grace-ma!" Joanna gasped, her hand over her mouth. "What did your parents say?"

"Believe it or not, they weren't too concerned. They knew it was just clothing." Grace shrugged. "I was still the same good kid. I was just reinventing my looks, not my *self*."

"What about Grandpa Doug? What did he say?"

Grandpa Doug.

Grace's high school boyfriend and later her husband, Dawn's father, and Joanna's grandfather. *Doug.* The sound of his name still made Grace smile.

Grace and Doug *had* to get married, although Grace was sure her granddaughter didn't know that part of her family's history. It was just the way things were back then. No one ever said it to her face, but Grace knew it was the talk of their small town. *A shotgun wedding.* That's what it would have been called.

Back in 1967 nice girls didn't go all the way. Not in small town New Jersey, they didn't. Fumbling backseat encounters that led to unplanned pregnancies were the turf of fishnet-stockinged girls with teased hair that smelled of cigarettes and their leather-jacketed boyfriends. Not *nice* girls. Not girls in Honors English who were headed off to college. Not girls like Grace Crawford.

Maybe it was inevitable. Grace and Doug met on the first day of high school as randomly assigned lab partners in freshman biology. He was a blue-eyed boy with smooth brown hair and an easy smile who dissected their frog while Grace snagged a hall pass and hid out in the girls' room. A promising beginning.

Study meetings became dates, and Grace began to decorate her brown paper book covers with their names framed within ink-drawn hearts. By their senior year "like" had turned into "love," and Grace dreamed of changing her name from Grace Crawford to Mrs. Douglas Raymond.

She just hadn't expected it to happen so quickly.

The night they graduated, two days before Grace left for San Francisco, she and Doug progressed from "almost" to "going all the way." By the time the leaves changed from green to orange, she knew she was pregnant, and before the year ended, Grace Crawford became Mrs. Douglas Raymond.

Dawn was born in the spring.

"Actually, Grandpa Doug liked my new style. He started calling me his 'little hippie girlfriend'. But remember, in our little town, it was all new back then. By the following year though, all the girls were sewing patches on their jeans, and the boys were growing their hair long."

"But still, living here wasn't like being in San Francisco. I mean it wasn't just about the clothes."

"That's for sure!" Grace chuckled. "Chester Grove, New Jersey was nothing like San Francisco, and you're right that it wasn't only about the clothes." She tilted her head and clicked her tongue. "But things were changing everywhere. Even here."

"Did you ever want to go back there though? To live?"

Had she ever wanted to go back there? To live? A simple

question. But the truth? The truth was...Grace didn't even know the truth. Wetting her lips, she breathed in, then out, and formulating an answer, came up with a single word.

"No."

"No?" Joanna asked, turning her grandmother's answer into a question.

"No." Grace shook her head. "I decided to marry Grandpa Doug, and we had your mother. We made a good life here." She squeezed Joanna's hand, an it's-the-truth gesture.

And they had made a good life. Grace and Doug had both grown up in Chester Grove. After graduating from high school, Doug worked in his parents' hardware store, and when his father retired, he took it over, keeping the property until his own retirement many years later. With a baby on the way, Grace's college plans were postponed, but after enrolling as a part-time student, she did eventually earn her degree. All in all, her summer in San Francisco had been no more than that. A single summer in San Francisco.

"Now, let's get to work," she said. "I'll put the pictures in order, and then we'll decide on the labels and decorations. Okay?"

"Okay." Joanna nodded, her dark brown eyes meeting her grandmother's.

Those eyes. So beautiful. Almost hypnotic. And so different from the greens and blues in Grace and Doug's families. Where did she get them? Joanna's father had brown eyes, although his were much lighter than hers.

Still, she must have gotten them from him.

Grace pushed her chair back and stood up, bending over the checkerboard of photos. Sliding, moving, and rearranging, she grouped the pictures into her best recollection of that long ago summer's chronology. Touristy pictures of

Paula and herself mugging for the camera in Union Square, eating ice cream on Fisherman's Wharf, and poking their heads out of a red cable car. Haight-Ashbury shots of braless girls wearing Indian print skirts and guys with beards sporting suede fringed vests.

But then, Grace's fingers stopped, and she snatched up a single picture, its colors faded, its surface dull. A row house walk-up, nine shallow steps leading up to its double front doors, Victorian in style. Her mouth grew dry, and her head started to pound.

"This doesn't belong here," she said, pushing the photo to the edge of the table.

"Why not?" Joanna reached for the picture. "What is it?"

Grace tucked her hands under her thighs and gripped the edge of her chair. A faux sneeze and a fake cough bought her a moment to think. "Just a house," she said, keeping her voice calm. "It wasn't even taken in San Francisco."

"Really? Where was it?"

"Actually, it's from Boston. I took a trip there with my parents years ago."

Joanna stared down at the picture. "Hmm, the architecture looks like San Francisco."

"Let me see," Grace took the picture and forced herself to look at it. "You're right. The architecture does look similar. But you can find Victorian row houses in lots of places. Boston, Washington––"

"And San Francisco," Joanna said.

"Yes, and San Francisco. That probably explains how it got into this pile. Anyway, it isn't important enough to be in the scrapbook." Pressing her lips together, Grace dropped the photo into the empty supply box.

"I wonder why you took it then." Joanna drummed her

fingers on the table. "Did somebody famous live there?" Her eyes widened.

"No, nobody famous lived there," Grace said quickly. "I must have just...I don't know...." She lifted her shoulders into what she hoped passed for a casual shrug. "I really don't remember why I took it."

"Okay, then why don't we start with this one?" Joanna pointed to the photo of her grandmother in the polka-dotted dress. "How do you want to caption it?"

Grace and Joanna spent the afternoon cutting, taping, and gluing, ultimately dedicating four lovingly created scrapbook pages to Grace's summer in San Francisco.

"We done good, Grace-ma," Joanna said, lifting her hand in a high five.

Grace met Joanna's palm with her own. "We always do!"

Joanna laughed and grabbed her jacket. Grace pulled her poncho over her head, and stepping onto the porch, they made their way down the stone path and into the car.

Just as they reached the bottom of the driveway, Joanna, in the passenger seat, turned to her grandmother. "Grace-ma, what ever happened to your friend, Paula? Are you still in touch with her?"

Grace's hands tightened on the steering wheel, and her mouth went dry. She swallowed. "N-no, not really."

And until yesterday, that was indeed true.

"Why not?"

Grace cleared her throat and wet her lips. "After she moved, our lives went in different directions, and we drifted apart."

That was definitely true.

"Do you ever miss her?"

"No, I really don't."

Another honest response.

"I've had...I *have*...a very full life." Grace took her right hand off the steering wheel and squeezed her granddaughter's thigh. "You, your mother, your father, and your grandfather when he was alive...I've been very lucky. Paula was a part of my past, and that was a long, long time ago." She blinked once, then focused her eyes on the road ahead. "It happens."

Back in her own house, alone, Grace reached into the bottom of her scrapbooking box and pulled out the picture of the old Victorian, not sure whether it was a thing to save or to destroy.

Holding it in her palm, she stared down at it. It was nothing more than a faded photograph. She carried it up the stairs and into her bedroom. Opening her jewelry box, she shoved it into the bottom drawer under a tangle of broken necklaces, mismatched earrings, and a brown plastic guitar pick.

D awn had set the table for just the two of them, herself and Joanna. It was a typical weekday night. Tom was away on business. Suburban life with a highly paid husband in a corporate job meant frequent travel and late nights at the office. That's what Dawn had signed on for when she'd married Tom, and she was used to it. Joanna was too.

Dawn cut into her baked lemon chicken. "Did you have a good time with Grace-ma today?" she asked her daughter.

"Yeah," Joanna said, mid-chew.

"What did you do?"

"Worked on the scrapbook."

"What sections?"

Joanna swallowed a mouthful of broccoli casserole and laid her fork across her plate. "Nineteen sixty-seven. Grace-ma's trip to San Francisco."

"Ah, the Summer of Love."

"Yeah," Joanna said, wiping her mouth with a napkin.

"How many pages did you finish?"

"Three."

"She's got some great pictures," Dawn said, trying one more time to turn the exchange into an actual conversation.

"Yeah," Joanna mumbled without looking up from her plate.

Dawn got the message. Her daughter wasn't in the mood to talk. So be it. Normal teenage stuff. She'd been there, done that. She remembered herself at fourteen. A freshman in high school trying to find her way, to figure out who she was. Fiercely protective of her privacy.

And she remembered her parents.

Dawn's father was the third generation and final owner of Raymond Hardware. Even after a Home Depot had opened up in the local strip mall, Doug's business still thrived. His customers would rather buy screwdrivers, ladders, and paint from the man with the perpetual smile who remembered the names of their children and grand-children than from the behemoth a few miles away. When he finally did retire, the Chamber of Commerce honored him with a farewell dinner, and the mayor himself shared memories of his own youthful summers spent working at Raymond Hardware under Doug's kind and careful tutelage.

As his daughter, Dawn was lucky to have been blessed with a father who was there to wipe away her childhood tears when she wanted him to, but who also knew when it was time to step back and give his daughter space. And privacy. As the saying goes, he gave her roots and wings. It was easy to be his child.

On the other hand, Dawn's mother was the perpetual hippie. In the eighties when all the other moms were outfitted in stirrup pants and oversized shirts with shoulder pads, she wore flare leg jeans and peasant shirts. In a land-scape of teased and permed hair, Grace Raymond kept hers long and straight.

"Dawn, your mom is so-o-o cool!" her friends would say, their words tinged with envy.

Then maybe you should try being her daughter. That was what Dawn wanted to tell them. Just once. But instead, she'd press her mouth into a Mona Lisa smile and shrug.

All Dawn wanted was for her mother to look, and more importantly, to *act* like all the other regular, average, and definitely "uncool" mothers of her friends. None of them could ever imagine that the go-with-the-flow, bohemian-looking woman whom they so admired routinely read her daughter's diaries, eavesdropped on her conversations, and searched through her closets and drawers.

One day after school, finding the shoes at the bottom of her closet rearranged, Dawn confronted her mother and asked her what she had been looking for. Grace's answer, if you could call it that, was that mothers worry and Dawn would understand when she had her own child.

Well, now that Dawn did have her own child, no, she didn't understand. But she did forgive. What Dawn couldn't wrap her head around was how close Joanna and Grace had become. They both loved all that sixties stuff––the music, the clothes...

It was more than that though. Dawn knew it was a good thing, for both her mother and her daughter, but sometimes she found herself wondering what it was they talked about. Maybe it was some sort of alternate generation bonding kind of thing. Still, she couldn't help but be a tiny bit jealous.

She blinked, shooing the thought away, and looked at her daughter. "Dessert?" she asked. "I've got––"

"Nah, I'm stuffed." Joanna patted her stomach. She pushed her chair back and scooped up their silverware and dishes.

Dawn watched as her daughter, her shiny dark hair cascading in a smooth waterfall down her back, carried them to the sink.

Stepping behind her, Dawn squeezed her shoulder. "I'll do them, hon. You can get started on your homework."

"Okay. Thanks, Mom," Joanna said and headed up the stairs to her room.

Dawn heard the bedroom door close as she scraped their plates into the garbage disposal.

Homework. Yeah, Joanna did need to get that done. She slid her English notebook out of her backpack and pulled out the list of literary terms that would be on tomorrow's test. *Metaphor, simile, allusion, irony, foreshadowing*...blah, blah, blah. Nothing she didn't already know. That meant all she'd have to do for the next day would be to translate a page of Spanish sentences and finish *Romeo and Juliet*. No biggie.

A bunch of people had asked her to join their homework groups. They divided up assignments and shared work. It was definitely unethical, but that wasn't the reason Joanna hadn't been interested. She didn't need anyone else to do her bio lab reports or geometry worksheets. Plus, she'd probably spend more time correcting their mistakes than she would doing it herself. Why bother? School work had always been easy for her, although she'd learned a long time ago not to let anyone know just how easy it truly was.

Back in elementary school, the guidance counselor had approached her parents about grade-skipping her. But why would Joanna have wanted to do that? Make things harder for herself? Forget about it. She knew she couldn't use her own laziness as a reason for nixing the idea. So, for a few days after dinner, she stuck her finger down her throat and made herself throw up. That, along with setting her alarm for 3:00 A.M. in order to wake up from an invented nightmare, was enough to keep her where she was.

Even back then, Joanna Harvey had already learned that high intelligence had uses far beyond the classroom.

4

W ith the scrapbook tucked under her arm, her cell phone in her pocket, and a mug of tea in her hand, Grace stepped out onto her front porch. The evening air was sparked with a hint of the chill promised by the arrival of fall. Grace had always liked the few weeks when the seasons were in flux––not quite one thing, but not yet the other. In another month, the temperature would drop, and instead of heading out to the porch, she would be sipping her after-dinner tea cocooned within the soft armchair nestled in the corner of her den, an afghan draped over her legs.

Grace set her mug and the scrapbook down on the wicker side table and settled into the porch swing, sinking into its cushions and leaning back. She sat in the center seat, leaving an empty spot on either side of her. Until four years ago, when she had lost Doug to a heart attack, quick and deadly, the left seat had been his, and the right was hers. They would share the center cushion, her legs draped over his. She had tried laying across the swing, her body covering its whole length, but it hadn't felt right. Doug's spot, in their home and in Grace's life, was now forever empty.

Leaning over the table, Grace took a quick sip of tea and reached for the scrapbook. She flipped through page after page, gently fingering the Polaroid photos, old birthday cards, faded Girl Scout badges, and the pressed corsage stapled onto a picture of herself with Doug at their senior prom that documented the first eighteen years of her life.

The following four pages, which she and Joanna had just created, immortalized her post-graduation trip to San Francisco. Gently bending the first page of the section over the last, she positioned the two airport photos of herself side by side. In the six weeks since she'd been away from home, the most obvious change was in her clothing and the length of her growing-out bangs.

Grace leaned over the book and peered closely first at one picture, then at the other. Her smile was the same. But her eyes...In six weeks, the expression in her eyes had gone from wide and open to slightly narrowed and darkly opaque. Maybe it was the lighting. She lifted the book, bringing it closer to her face, and stared at the pictures. No, it wasn't the lighting.

Doug never knew he had saved her, and he had saved Dawn too. Grace hadn't thanked him. Not then, not ever. She couldn't. Because if she had, then she would have had to tell him...no, never mind. None of that mattered anymore. It was a long time ago, and she hadn't thought about...

But Paula's letter had changed things.

She looked up at the darkening sky and rubbed the back of her neck. Might as well get it over with. She shook out her hands and pulled her phone out of her pocket. With a shaky finger, she tapped in Paula's number. It rang. One, two, three times...

"Hello?" the familiar voice answered.

"Paula, it's Grace."

"Gracie! I was hoping you'd call. It's been such a long time, and I...well...How are you?"

"I'm good, Paula. How are you?"

"I'm fine these days," she said. "I did have a rough few years a while back. Maybe that was after we lost touch. I don't know how much you..." Her loud sigh pushed its way through the phone and into Grace's ear. "Never mind though. Everything's okay now. I even have a job with the SPCA. It's administrative, but I get to work with the animals sometimes, and..." She stopped. "But what about you? The last time we talked Joanna was a baby. She must be...what? A teenager by now? And how's Dawn?"

"Yes, Joanna is fourteen. Can you believe it? She's wonderful. And Dawn and Tom are great. It's hard to know where to begin--"

"I know." Paula giggled. "We have a lot to catch up on. But listen, I reached out to you because I'm going to New York for Joey's daughter's wedding in a couple of weeks. He's sending a car for me, but I can hang out at the Port Authority for a few hours. So, I was thinking maybe you could meet me, and--"

"Of course, I can meet you," Grace said. "Just give me the information, and I'll be there."

"That would be great. I really want to see you, Gracie."

"Me too, Paula. Me too," Grace said, gifting her with the *correct* response. True or not.

"And bring pictures," Paula said. "Okay?"

They settled on a plan, arranged the details, and said good-bye. And just like that, Grace had agreed to see the one person who knew the secret she had kept locked away from the world and even from her own family, especially from her own family, for more than fifty years.

Could she have said no? Should she have? Grace supposed she could have made up an excuse, maybe a previous commitment or an appointment that couldn't be canceled, but Paula...Paula would never have taken no for an answer. If she wanted to see Grace, she would have figured out a way to do it.

It did make sense though. Paula was going to be in New York. It was just a bus ride away.

But still...

Closing the scrapbook, Grace moved it back to the side table. She slid her afghan up from her lap, wrapping it tightly around her shoulders, and reached for her tea. The mug had grown cold.

5

A glass of orange juice and a bowl of milk-drenched Rice Krispies. Joanna's typical Saturday morning breakfast. Her mother was at the supermarket, and her father was in Shanghai. Or maybe it was Hong Kong. She wasn't sure. Anyway, he'd be home tomorrow. Probably not for long though. Tom Harvey was a partner in a consulting firm, and his clients were corporations not people. Joanna didn't know exactly what he did, but he spent lots of time on planes and made plenty of money.

The silence of the house was broken only by the snap-crackle-pop of Joanna's cereal. She was a bit bored at the moment, but something would come up. It always did. As she reached for her orange juice, her cell phone rang, Erin's name lighting up the screen.

A phone call, not a text. Good. Joanna had let her girls know that she preferred calls. Too much could be misunderstood on text. And the thought of saving written conversations? *Her* written conversations? That was *not* happening. Plus, she didn't want to be annoyed with the beep-beep-beep of a constantly chirping phone. Her girls could do it among themselves, but not with her. *She* expected a call. It had taken a while for the girls to get used to it, but eventually they did. They had to.

Erin asked Joanna if she'd rather go to the movies, the mall, or bowling. She'd already texted with Megan and Paige. They were leaving it up to Joanna.

As they should.

"Bowling? You know I don't like bowling," Joanna said.

"It wasn't my idea." Erin coughed, then sniffed. "Paige suggested it."

Joanna pushed her breath out in a loud huff. She knew Erin heard it.

She waited.

"So..." Erin finally said, breaking the icy silence.

"So...why didn't you *remind* Paige that I don't like bowling?"

"I-I should have, Joanna. You're right. I wasn't thinking," Erin said. "I'm sorry," she added quietly.

"Okay, Erin. Just tell them we'll go to the mall. My mom's not home, so I don't have a ride."

"That's okay. We can pick you up. In an hour or so?"

"No, that's not good for me."

"O-okay. So, what time do you think?"

Joanna plunked a spoonful of cereal into her mouth and chewed. She swallowed slowly. "Two hours."

"Okay," Erin said.

Joanna clicked off the phone, her good-bye understood. She didn't really need two hours. But she was annoyed. Her girls knew she didn't like bowling. So...

Anyway, it didn't matter. They'd pick her up in two hours. Just as she had instructed.

She finished her breakfast, washed and put away her dishes, and dressed. Flare leg jeans, a long flowy top, hoop earrings, and a silver cuff bracelet. Pulling out her copy of *Stranger in a Strange Land*, she opened it to the bookmarked page and began to read.

~

The mall was...well, it was the mall. Moms with strollers, groups of wandering teenagers trying to occupy themselves on a Saturday afternoon, and the random thirty-something woman on a mission for the perfect shoe, pair of jeans, lipstick, or whatever. Joanna, Erin, Megan, and Paige were in the "wandering teenager" category. Flitting in and out of stores, they flipped through racks of clothing, leafed through fashion magazines, devoured samples from the candy shop, and dabbed their wrists with perfume roller-balls. At the food court, they snagged a front table with a good view all around.

Joanna held the table, and the others drifted past the drink vending machines, the sub shop, and the Chinese place, stopping at the long line snaking up to the McDonald's counter. Megan pointed to the menu board, and Paige shook her head and grabbed Erin's elbow. Megan's eyebrows shot up, and her face turned pink. Paige said something Joanna couldn't hear and pulled on Erin's arm, steering her toward the vending machines. Megan didn't move from her spot on the McDonald's line, but turned her head to stare at her friends' narrow backs. Joanna closed her eyes and shook her head. Just one more mini-drama.

Paige and Erin, carrying vending machine bottles of water, claimed the chairs across from Joanna. Erin leaned over and handed her one of the bottles.

Megan, clutching a bright red box of French fries and holding a large cup against her chest, scurried over and plopped into the chair next to Joanna. "Sorry about that," she said, holding out the box of fries. "Anybody want some?"

Joanna shook her head, and a millisecond later Paige and Erin did the same.

Megan shrugged, her pink face deepening to red. "I didn't have lunch," she mumbled and pushed a clump of fries into her mouth.

Even with her shoulders hunched forward and her back rounded against the chair, Megan's chest strained against the fabric of her shirt. Such a pretty face, if only she'd... Actually, Megan wasn't really fat. Ten pounds would have done it. But as long as she kept eating those French fries...

Paige stared at Megan, her partly open mouth exposing her braces. Catching Joanna's eye, she quickly snapped her mouth shut. Even without looking below the table, Joanna knew Paige's hands were tucked under her thighs. If she sat like that in school instead of letting her arm pop up like bread in a toaster every time a teacher asked a question *and* if she didn't have braces, she could have been leading her own band of wannabes instead of trailing after Joanna. But she wouldn't be wearing braces much longer.

Joanna needed to keep a close watch on her.

Erin sipped her water and stared at the escalator. Her mom had driven the girls to the mall today, probably grilling her daughter with a bunch of who?-what?-where? questions before she gave her the okay. But as long as Erin was with Joanna, the straight-A, "good girl" kind of friend that was a mother's dream, her mom wouldn't have had a problem. *Ha!*

All at once, a pink flush spread across Paige's face, and Erin's eyes went wide. They both stared, laser focused, at a spot somewhere above Joanna's head. Feeling two quick tugs on her hair, Joanna turned around in her chair and looked up into Ryan Hunter's grin.

"Hey," he said.

That's original, Joanna *didn't* say. Instead, she matched his smile and his choice of greeting. "Hey."

"So, what's going on?" he asked.

"Not much." Joanna shrugged. "Just hanging." She tilted her head sideways in a half-turn back to the table. "Ryan, this is Erin, Paige, and Megan." She pointed at each of them, her finger bobbing in an arc around the table.

The girls curved their mouths into friendly, but not too-friendly smiles.

Ryan nodded, his floppy brown hair falling across his forehead and offered them a communal "Hey."

This guy had some vocabulary, Joanna thought, clasping her hands in her lap and willing herself not to roll her eyes.

Then, looking at Joanna, *only* at Joanna, Ryan placed a hand on the back of her chair and leaned over. His breath was minty. Pleasant enough. But still, he was too close.

"So, Joanna, I'm having some people over tonight. Wanna come?"

Joanna didn't ask him who his "people" were. She already knew. Brett and Matt, maybe Dan, Emily and Sarah for sure. They were the popular kids––juniors, two years older than Joanna and her crew. She could tell he thought she should be flattered. He had that smirky kind of grin on his face.

Joanna pushed her lips into a girlish pout. "But Ryan, I'm with my friends today."

"You can bring 'em," he said with a trying-to-look-casual shrug. He stretched his mouth into a wider smile, but his light gray eyes turned dark.

Easy to control a mouth. Eyes were tougher.

Joanna mimicked his shrug. "Okay. We'll see. I'm not sure what's going on yet."

Ryan took his arm off her chair and stepped back. "Alright then. I gotta get going. Brett's waiting downstairs." He tugged her hair again and turned toward the escalator. "See you later," he called over his shoulder.

Joanna smiled and waved.

Elbows on the table, Erin, Paige, and Megan all leaned toward her. Joanna angled her chair to face the anxiously waiting trio.

"So, are we going?" Paige asked.

"I can go if I tell my mom it's at your house," Erin said, her eyes on Joanna.

Joanna reached across the table, snatched up one of Megan's fries, and popped it into her mouth. Chewing, she shook her head. The girls, *her* girls, stared at her. She swallowed and slowly ran her tongue over her lips.

"I'm not really in the mood right now," she said. "Maybe another time. But you guys can go. Don't let me stop you."

"C'mon, Joanna. He asked *you*. We were the add-ons." Paige's voice was even, but her nostrils flared.

"Nah, not tonight. Another time maybe." Joanna grabbed another fry from Megan.

And just like that, she showed them. She could open doors, and she could close them too.

Paige's eyebrows scrunched down over her eyes, and her mouth pressed into a thin, hard line. Joanna lowered her own eyebrows and squeezed her lips together, mirroring Paige's expression, and stared at her. A thin bluish vein on the side of Paige's forehead began to pulse, and she reached for her water.

Keeping her eyes on Paige as she gulped from the bottle, Joanna smiled when she put it down and brought her left wrist to her nose. She sniffed loudly. "I like this," she said, tapping her rollerball-scented wrist.

Megan leaned toward Joanna. "What is it?"

"Marc Jacobs."

"Which Marc Jacobs?" Erin asked.

"Good question. It's the one called 'Daisy'. I like it." Joanna sniffed her wrist again. "I like it a lot. Let's go back to Sephora. I want to put some more on." She stood and pushed her chair in.

Erin jumped up, and Megan and Paige turned toward her, their heads swiveling as if on cue. Megan popped her last fry into her mouth, crumpled the empty box, and stood. Paige looked up from her seat, her gaze shifting from Erin to Megan to Joanna. Her chest moved up and down as she breathed in and out, her mouth closed. With a loud sigh, she stood up slowly.

"Let's go," Joanna said. Turning on her heel, she power walked out of the food court, not looking to see if the others were behind her.

She didn't have to.

Joanna strode into Sephora and headed directly to the rollerball display. Plucking the "Daisy" sample from its slot, she touched it to her wrists and behind each of her ears. She fluttered her arms through the air like a pair of graceful birds, then held her wrist up to Erin's nose. "What do you think?"

Erin breathed in. "I like it," she said. "It smells good on you."

"Megan?" Joanna lifted her wrist to Megan's face.

"Mmm...delicious," Megan said, inhaling.

Joanna turned to Paige, who stood motionless, watching. "Wanna smell?" She held out her hand, wrist up.

Paige shrugged and bent to sniff Joanna's wrist. "It's good," she said, lifting her head. "But you really can't tell until it dries down. About twenty minutes."

Joanna stepped back and crossed her arms over her chest. "Well, *I* like it," she said. "Anyway, I need to go to the ladies' room. You guys wait here, and I'll meet you up front in a few minutes." Turning on her heel, she walked out of the store.

In the restroom, Joanna pulled out her phone and moved through another level of Candy Crush. She didn't know what the big deal was about this game, but it did pass the time. She ran a brush through her hair and headed back to Sephora.

They should be ready by now.

Ten minutes after Megan called her mother to pick them up, the girls made their way out of the mall, positioning themselves in a row along the brick wall marking its main entrance.

"Hey Joanna, before my mom gets here, we got you a present," Megan said, digging into her bag. She pulled her hand out, closed into a fist.

Joanna raised her eyebrows and leaned over.

Megan opened her hand, uncovering a gold-capped rollerball decorated with painted white daisies. She smiled, extending it to Joanna. "It's from all of us."

"Thank you," Joanna said, plucking the tube from Megan's hand and dropping it into her own bag. "Thank you all." She looked at Megan, then Erin, and then Paige, nodding and returning each of their smiles.

No receipt, no box. The rollerball sample was almost full.

It had been a good day.

Megan's mom stopped her car in front of the wide bank of flagstone steps leading up to Joanna's house. Thanking her for the ride and with a communal "talk to you later" tossed out to her girls, Joanna climbed the steps and fit her key into the lock. With one foot inside the house, the door still open, she turned back and watched the car continue down the other side of the circular driveway.

Joanna lived in a big house in a town of big houses. Hers might have been a bit taller, a bit wider, but it wasn't all that different from the others in Oakdale. It was the kind of house her mother had always wanted. And her father wanted to make her mother happy. So, it worked. For them. And for Joanna too. Closing the door and stepping inside, Joanna heard her mother's voice singing out from the kitchen.

"Joanna, is that you?"

Looking up from her laptop as her daughter entered the kitchen, Dawn smiled. "How was the mall?"

"Fine." Joanna shrugged and stepped behind Dawn, leaning over her mother's shoulder and peering down at her open laptop. "What are you doing?"

"Just going over Dad's reunion invitation," Dawn said. "Thirty years. It's a big one."

"You're editing it?"

"Just a little," Dawn said quickly. "Here and there."

Joanna plopped down onto the chair next to her mother and planted her elbows on the kitchen table. Tilting her head and fixing Dawn with her dark-eyed stare, she dropped her chin onto her clasped hands. She didn't speak, and Dawn felt her face grow warm under her daughter's gaze.

"So..." Dawn said, breaking the silence with a single word.

Not a question, not a statement. Just a word.

"So, if it's for Dad's college reunion, why are *you* writing the invitation?"

"I'm not *writing* it, Joanna. I'm just making some minor suggestions. Your father's on the alumni board and the reunion committee. And he's busy at work too. You know the hours he puts in, plus the travel. He won't even be home from Shanghai until tomorrow." Dawn sighed. "And this is not a big deal for me to do."

"It's okay, Mom." Joanna held up her hands. A mock surrender. "I get it."

But Dawn knew she didn't "get it." She was well aware that her daughter saw her as someone who had made a mistake by trading in her own corporate job in the city for life as a stay-at-home mom in the suburbs. Someone who threw her college degree down the toilet. Someone who gave up her own life to serve the needs of her husband and child. She didn't seem to understand or to accept the fact that that decision had been made by Dawn alone, who counted herself lucky to have a husband who was able and willing to allow her to live the way she did. It was a gift, not a sacrifice.

And the fact that Joanna looked at her grandmother's life through different glasses than she used for hers chafed at Dawn like a tiny pebble in her shoe. Just because Grace still dressed like a flower child and lived in a house filled with macramé and pottery didn't mean she hadn't made sacrifices by settling down in her hometown with her high school sweetheart instead of running back to Paula and her hippie friends in San Francisco.

Dawn had always suspected there was more to her mother's story than a teenage pregnancy and a youthful marriage. And although Grace never wanted her daughter to have secrets, Dawn had the feeling that even after all these years, her mother still had a few of her own.

Was she curious? Of course, she was. She'd often wondered about the disconnect between her mother's free-and-easy, go-with-the-flow appearance and her single-minded mission to dig into every nook and cranny of her daughter's adolescent life. But for Dawn, respect for privacy, whether it was for her mother's or her daughter's, trumped curiosity, and it always would.

She smiled at her daughter. "So, did you get anything at the mall?"

~

Did you get anything at the mall?

"No, not today." The answer to her mother's question rolled off Joanna's tongue.

Dawn's mouth stayed relaxed, but her eyes flashed with a flicker of disappointment. Like most people, she was easy to read. Joanna just needed to watch their eyes. That's where the truth lived. She knew her mother would have liked her to buy the clothes that every other high school girl seemed to be wearing, but too-tight jeans and designer workout wear didn't do it for her.

Then again, maybe Dawn would have been happy to hear that her daughter had in fact gotten something from the mall, a little *gift* from her friends. Joanna kept her expression neutral as the thought flitted across her mind.

Perhaps she should have reached into her bag and pulled out the perfume rollerball her girls had somehow "picked up" for her. *Literally.* Yeah, her mother would have just *loved* that.

"Maybe next time then," Dawn said, unwittingly breaking into Joanna's mischievous reverie.

"I don't need anything, Mom," she answered with a delicious-to-herself mock innocence.

"Okay, Joanna." Dawn nodded with practiced patience. "That's up to you, but if you––"

"I know," Joanna said, mimicking her mother's slow nod. "And thank you," she added.

Always the polite daughter.

Dawn changed the subject, jumping to the next step in their conversational dance. "So, do you have plans for tonight?"

Plans? Hmmm...That might be a good idea.

"Yeah, actually I do," Joanna said. "I just need to make some calls."

Perched on her bed, Joanna leaned over her night table and slid open the bottom drawer. She reached into the back and pulled out the sponge-painted jewelry box she had decorated for a long ago camp project. Flipping the top open, she turned the box over, letting its contents spill out onto her bed.

A bottle of a nude colored nail polish, a minty lip gloss, a rainbow-shaped eraser, an orange and yellow Koosh ball, a zebra-striped letter *J* dangling from a metal key ring. A hodgepodge of "gifts" that she certainly didn't need and had never really wanted. The pilfered collection was merely a vehicle––a way of seeing what her girls would do for her.

She pulled the perfume rollerball out of her bag, dropping it into her open palm. Pretty bottle. She wondered who had actually taken it. Was it Erin, the peacemaker? Megan, the chubby girl "with such a pretty face?" Or was it Paige, the not-as-smart-as she-thinks-she-is troublemaker? No matter. They were all in on it.

So, about tonight? The girls probably did deserve a little something.

Ryan's party? No, bad idea. She had already said no to that. And it was a much bigger reward than she felt like giving them anyway.

Plus, Paige was really bugging her. It wasn't that the girl had actually said or done anything. It was the look on her face, her expressions––like she was challenging Joanna or something. And Paige *knew* she didn't like bowling.

She tapped the gold-capped tip of the rollerball against her cheek. Maybe...yeah...

Joanna dropped the perfume onto her bed, adding it to her collection of trinkets. Using both hands, she swept the whole mess into her jewelry box and snapped the lid closed. Then snatching up her cell phone, she called Erin.

"J-Joanna?" Erin's voice was shaky, unsure.

Joanna knew exactly what was going through Erin's mind...

It's not like Joanna to call right after we've been together all afternoon. Is she upset? Did I do something wrong?

Joanna cleared her throat, drawing out the moment. "Listen, Erin, I'm having a sleepover tonight," she said. "Dinner at my house. Let the others know."

Drumming her fingers against the side of her knee, her mouth stretched into a smile.

6

"**G**irls, I'm leaving," Dawn called out, poking her head into the stairway leading down to the basement.

The gritty wail of Janis Joplin's voice was the only response that made its way up the stairs.

Two generations later, Joanna had fallen in love with the music that had captivated her grandmother. From psychedelic rock to bluesy jams to sweet harmonies, she feasted on them all. And from what Dawn could hear, it sounded like she was spreading the love, leading her friends back in musical time.

Joanna had always been a leader. Without even trying, she had the others following her around like she was their own personal Pied Piper.

"Girls," Dawn repeated, louder this time.

Same answer––the music.

She made her way down the stairs and knocked on the closed basement door. A sound of approaching footsteps broke through the musical din, and the door swung open.

"You can come in," Joanna said, stepping back.

Erin, Megan, and Paige, sitting cross-legged on the floor, their backs pressed into the couch, looked up at Dawn like smiling triplets. Footage from Woodstock, the camera panning the sea of concert-goers who had helped make history, filled the screen. It was the same DVD Joanna had watched over and over. Dawn raised her eyebrows and looked at her daughter.

"Yes, I put it on again." Joanna lifted her chin and nodded. "It's history. A cultural phenomenon."

A cultural phenomenon? Impressive terminology for a fourteen-year-old.

"Yes, it is." Dawn nodded. "Anyway, I'm leaving for dinner with Lisa." She turned toward Joanna's trio of friends. "I left a lasagna in the fridge for you to microwave. And I'll be home late, so don't wait up." She winked.

A chorus of thanks and giggles was their communal answer.

"Have fun, Mom," Joanna said. "And say 'hi' to Aunt Lisa."

"Will do." Dawn blew a kiss into the room and closed the door behind her.

Dawn's night out with Lisa followed a familiar game plan, one that was special and sacred to both of them. They each made the forty-minute drive––okay, maybe fifty minutes for Lisa––to *Monty's Bar and Grill*, where they ordered food and wine, and settled in for an all-night dinner filled with laughter and the type of conversation they could only have with each other. They'd been best friends for so many years that they spoke in shorthand. No backstory necessary.

"My friend will be here soon." Dawn smiled at the waiter. "Just water for now."

Always prepared for the perpetually "so sorry I'm late" Lisa, she cracked open her book and chuckled.

Just as Dawn turned the last page in the chapter, Lisa burst into the restaurant and rushed over to the table.

"So sorry I'm late," she said, shrugging off her jacket and plopping into the chair across from Dawn.

"No problem," Dawn said, closing her book and swallowing a giggle.

"I just couldn't get out of the apartment," Lisa said. "Sometimes I feel like I'm becoming my mother." She shuddered, shaking her head in a quick back and forth motion. "Homework before TV. Clean your room. I don't care what everyone else is allowed to do." Her words came out in a hoarse bark. "And the best..." She leaned over, pressing her hands into the table. "Because I'm your mother!" she hissed.

Dawn exploded into the kind of laughter that brought tears to her eyes and made her shoulders bob up and down. Even back when they were kids, Lisa could do that to her. Whether she was imitating their gym teacher's ape-like walk or their Brownie leader's high-pitched giggle, she would have Dawn hiccuping with laughter in seconds.

They had both left small town New Jersey for college, but unlike Dawn, Lisa had made her exodus permanent. These days she managed to juggle a full-time job in pharmaceutical sales, motherhood, and marriage to an always-on-call obstetrician.

Dawn was in awe. Unlike her friend, she had married a New York guy who had always dreamed of raising his children in small town suburbia. Backyard barbecues and neighbors you know, the whole bit. Monthly dinners (girls only) kept both Dawn and Lisa sane.

The waiter brought menus, but the women didn't need them. Grilled salmon for Dawn, chicken piccata for Lisa, and a glass of chardonnay for each of them.

"But seriously Dawn, don't you ever find yourself acting like your mother? When you're dealing with Joanna?"

"*My* mother?" Dawn's body stiffened, her shoulders pressing into the back of her chair. "Grace?"

"Whoa, Dawn," Lisa said, raising her hands. "It wasn't an insult. Just a question."

"I'm sorry. Just a visceral reaction, I guess."

Lisa pressed her lips together and nodded, and Dawn knew her friend understood. Back when they were teenagers, Lisa was the one who had come up with one of the many hiding places for Dawn's diary—a ripped backpack stashed at the bottom of her closet. She was the one Dawn cried to each time they would hear the soft click of the downstairs phone extension being picked up during one of their conversations. Dawn was a good kid, but her mother never respected her privacy. Never. And Lisa, more than anyone, knew that.

"I'm sure I've made mistakes with Joanna, but not the same ones my mother made with me. I came up with my own." Dawn shrugged and laughed. Then, her face turned serious. "I trust my daughter, and I want her to know it. I give her space," she said. "But the strangest thing to me is how close she's become to my mother. I don't get it."

"You've said that before. What do you mean?"

Pulling her bottom lip into her mouth, Dawn looked down at the tablecloth, then brought her gaze back to Lisa. She wasn't really sure what she'd meant. And that's exactly what she said.

Lisa's eyebrows arched, her eyes meeting Dawn's, and she waited, giving her friend time.

Dawn reached for her wineglass and took a thoughtful sip. "Look, it's normal to be close to a grandparent. That's a good thing, and I want that for my daughter. I want it for my mother too."

"I know you do. But I'm hearing a 'but' in there..."

"Yeah." Dawn clicked her tongue. "It's just that Joanna seems so wrapped up in the Sixties these days. The music, the clothes...I don't understand the fascination."

"Are you worried about drugs?"

"No, it's not that." Dawn shook her head. "She's not the type."

Lisa traced a circle around the base of her wineglass, then looked up at Dawn. "You sure?"

Dawn rolled her eyes and nodded. "I'm sure. And the reason is because, believe it or not, my hippie mother, whom Joanna idolizes, is more anti-drug than...uh...than..."

"The pope?"

"Yeah, the pope. That sounds good." Dawn laughed. "I assume he'd be against drugs, right?"

"I would assume so." Lisa pushed her lips together, her face mock serious.

"Plus, her friends aren't the type. They're nice girls, not the wild, popular ones." Dawn leaned toward Lisa, her elbows on the table. "And it's not sex I'm worried about either," she said, lowering her voice to a whisper.

"That was my next question. You know, Dawn, Joanna is a beauty. Truly. She looks like a young Ali MacGraw. Back when she was in that old movie *Love Story*. And her eyes? The boys are going to follow her anywhere. They probably already do."

"Thank you, Lisa." Dawn smiled at her dear friend. "But she really doesn't seem interested. She's never had a boyfriend. I guess she's not mature like that. Not yet anyway."

"That's my girl," Lisa said. "She's got plenty of time." She laid her hands flat on the table. "So then, what is it that you're worried about?"

"It's not that I'm worried. I just don't understand it." Dawn sighed. "I'll give you an example," she said. "Her three best friends are sleeping over tonight. And when I went down to say good-bye to them, Joanna had them all watching the Woodstock DVD. She must have seen it a dozen times already. Maybe they have too. And now, they're all wearing peasant shirts and bell-bottoms, just like Joanna does."

"Okay...?"

"I know. It sounds ridiculous, right?" Dawn asked, not waiting for an answer. "Maybe it's just that she's spending a lot of time with my mother. They're working together on a scrapbook of Mom's life, and I feel like...I don't know...I guess I just feel..." Dawn pushed her lips together, not wanting to say the word that had sprung into her head.

Jealous.

"Left out?" Lisa said, coming to her friend's rescue.

"Yeah, that's it. 'Left out'." Dawn seized on the less threatening choice of words. "I do feel left out."

"I get it, Dawn. I do. Teenage girls have complicated relationships with their mothers. I never know whether Chloe is going to treat me like the Wicked Witch of the West or her own personal fairy godmother." Lisa smirked. "I think their relationship with a grandmother is much easier. It's simpler."

Dawn tapped her chin and nodded slowly. "I guess you're right."

"Do you think Joanna's been confiding in your mother? Telling her things that you don't know?"

"No." Dawn shook her head. "Actually, I think it might be the opposite," she said, suddenly realizing the other issue that had been bothering her. The words tumbled out of her mouth. "My mother's always been a mystery to me. I know her summer in San Francisco was an important event in her life. That's the best word I can come up with right now." She lifted her fingers in air quotes. "'Event'. Anyway, she fell in love with the whole hippie scene—the clothes, the music, and I think maybe the lifestyle too. But she and my father had conceived *me* before she left, although neither of them knew it yet. Then later, when they realized she was pregnant, they got married. Joanna doesn't know that part. But they built a life together and had a wonderful marriage. They made it work, and I think they truly loved each other."

"I do too," Lisa said. "So...?"

"So, why didn't she ever want to go back to San Francisco? Even for a vacation? I remember my father suggesting it lots of times. It's almost as if my mother loves San Francisco and her Summer of Love, but only from afar. I think she has secrets, Lisa. I really do."

"And you think she might be sharing them with Joanna?"

"No, I don't. But I think Joanna is...I don't know exactly. It just seems like something's up with her, that she's..." Dawn's breath came out in a long sigh.

Smiling, Lisa held up a hand, ticking off a string of clichés on her fingers. "Trying to find herself? Figure out who she is? Searching for her identity?"

Dawn laughed. "Maybe you're right, Lisa." She shrugged and dug a fork into her salmon. "As if any of us knows who we really are..."

7

"I still can't believe your mom actually cooks for us. Mine orders in pizza," Erin said, plunging her fork into her lasagna, "if she even does that." She smirked, stopping her fork halfway to her mouth. "Usually she just tells me to invite you guys over *after* dinner."

"That's how most moms are. Mine too," Paige said. "Joanna's just lucky." She darted a sidelong glance at Joanna and then reached for her napkin.

Lucky. A throwaway word. A lucky guess, a lucky break, lucky stars. A word that didn't mean much. Not to Joanna. But coming from Paige, it sounded like fingernails on a blackboard. And *"just* lucky" was even worse. *Don't hate me because I'm beautiful.* Wasn't that a line from an old shampoo commercial?

What Joanna wanted to tell Paige was—*Don't hate me because I'm intelligent, have a mom who cooks, and am beautiful to boot.* That was luck, true. But what Joanna had done with it...that was her. *All* her.

And why shouldn't her mom cook dinner for her and

her friends? Her only job was to be a wife and a mother. Or did that count as two? Wife *and* mother? She had walked away from a corporate career and climbed onto the mommy track. It was totally her decision, her choice. Her mother wasn't like Grace-ma, who had found herself pregnant at eighteen and *had* to get married.

Back in those days, in her small town, Grace-ma did *have* to get married. Neither she nor Dawn had told Joanna the story, and they probably thought she didn't know. But after putting together her grandparents' wedding date with her mom's birthday, it hadn't been hard to figure out. Grace-ma hadn't had a lot of options though. Or *luck*. But Dawn did, and she had chosen her life.

Joanna, on the other hand, was going to *create* her life.

She stared at Paige. "Yeah, I guess I am...*lucky*." She tilted her head and smiled, mouth closed.

Paige nodded, her hands in her lap, and matched Joanna's semblance of a smile.

Erin put her fork down and pushed her plate away. "That was delicious," she said, patting her stomach.

"Mm-hmm," Megan managed to mumble, mid-chew. Her neck rippled as she quickly swallowed, and her eyes moved to the remaining lasagna cooling in the casserole dish. She leaned over the table, her breasts pushing into its edge.

Paige cleared her throat, and Megan pulled back.

Turning to her empty plate, Megan slowly pushed it away. "That's it for me," she said.

The girls cleared the table, loaded the dishwasher with their scraped-clean plates, and followed Joanna down to the basement.

"Let the night begin," Joanna said, smacking her lips together.

Erin and Megan claimed spots on the couch, sinking into the soft cushions, and Paige strode past them, positioning herself next to Joanna.

"Truth or Dare?" Paige asked, shifting her gaze from Erin to Megan and then back to Erin.

Megan kept her face neutral, but her tightly clenched hands anchored to her thighs told *her* truth, that of a chubby girl who had never been kissed and who did not want to play Truth or Dare. Not again.

Erin lifted her shoulders in an okay-if-you-want-to kind of shrug and looked to Joanna for an answer.

Truth or Dare? Why? They had already played it enough times for Joanna to know that Paige's left boob was bigger than her right one and that Erin cheated on math tests. She knew about Megan's lack of kissing experience and that her older sister stashed pot and pills at the bottom of her closet. She knew Paige's parents slept in separate bedrooms and that Erin's uncle had committed suicide. She even knew Erin had been a bedwetter. She had drawn a fake tattoo with permanent marker on Megan's thigh, watched Paige swallow five spoonfuls of mustard, and listened in on Erin's prank call to the mean old lady who lived down the street.

As for Joanna? The others had seen her naked, and they knew she had had sex with a guy in camp the previous summer. Bottom line––they knew just what Joanna wanted them to. Not more, not less. So no, Joanna did not want to play Truth or Dare. She had no reason to.

Besides, she had a different agenda for the evening.

"Actually, I have another idea," Joanna said softly, making Erin and Megan lean forward in order to hear her. "Something different." She turned to Paige and pointed to the couch. "Why don't you sit down?" she said, her question a command.

"Okay," Paige said and settled in next to Erin, crossing her arms in her lap.

Joanna flashed them all a smile, and drawing out the moment with a catlike stretch, she slowly turned toward the corner of the room, and in a lazy stroll, sauntered over to the mini-fridge squatting against the wall.

Feeling three pairs of eyes on her back, she opened the door and pulled out a foil-covered paper plate. Returning to her girls, she set the plate on the coffee table in front of them and lowered herself to the floor.

Their chins jutting forward and their shoulders hunched, the others stared at the plate. Joanna lifted the foil and unveiled four brownie squares arranged in a circle around a stack of neatly folded napkins.

She turned to Megan. "Remember last week? When I asked you to get some of your sister's weed?"

"Uh...you mean..." Megan pointed to the plate.

"Mm-hmm." Joanna nodded. "I did some baking yesterday."

Paige's mouth curved into a smile, and Erin bit down on her lip. Megan exhaled and leaned back into the couch.

"So, you guys up for this?' Joanna asked, not that she had to.

She knew her girls. Paige was always ready for anything, Erin was usually a little nervous, but willing to follow the others, and Megan was eager to please.

Paige punched her fist into the air. "Hell, yeah."

"I'll do it," Megan said.

"M-me too," Erin murmured.

Joanna pulled four water bottles from the fridge and handed each of the girls a brownie, saving the largest for herself. "I know you guys haven't done this before, so––"

"Did you?" Paige interrupted.

"Yeah," Joanna answered truthfully. Not that it was any of Paige's business.

Paige sucked in a sharp breath. "You did? When?"

"Last year when I went to visit my cousin in Colorado, we did edibles."

Joanna did *not* add that her heart had felt like it was going to explode or that she had truly believed the night-time rain was going to carry them away in a gigantic flood before they'd have time to build an ark. Nor did she mention that she'd spent an hour curled up in a fetal ball while her cousin held her hand and tried to talk her down. She didn't say that she would never allow herself to feel that vulnerable, that out of control, again. In other words, Joanna didn't tell the girls that edible marijuana was not for her. Not then. Not ever.

She needed to be in control. Always.

And she certainly didn't tell them that the biggest brownie, the one she had claimed for herself, was just *that*. A brownie. Nor did she point out that the brownie she had handed to Paige was extra, extra special, and that Joanna had made it just for her.

"But as I was saying," she continued, avoiding Paige's eyes, "edible pot is stronger than smoked, and it'll take at least half an hour for you to feel anything. Maybe longer. It can be pretty intense, so if any of you don't want to do it––"

"I want to," Paige interrupted. Again.

Megan nodded. "I'm in," she said.

"Me too," Erin said quietly.

"Good," Joanna said, bringing her hands together in a single clap. "Bon appétit!"

She bit into her brownie and chewed, watching as the others followed her lead, just like they always did.

"Not bad," Megan mumbled, her mouth full.

Paige wrinkled her nose. "I guess," she said.

Erin ate in small bites and punctuated her swallows with swigs of water.

The girls finished their brownies and swept the crumbs, napkins, plate and crumpled foil into the trash.

"So, what do we do now?" Megan asked.

Paige clamped her hands to her hips and rolled her eyes. "What do you think we do, Megan?" Her breath came out in a huff. "We wait."

Megan pushed her lips together, and her cheeks turned pink. Crossing her legs, she looked down at the floor.

"Whoa," Joanna said, her hands held up, a double stop sign. "We don't have to just wait."

She reached down below the coffee table and slid open the single drawer built into its base. Scooping up the stack of coloring books and bucket of crayons she'd stowed inside, she dropped them onto the table.

"Help yourselves, guys," she said, snatching up a book of swirling paisley designs for herself.

The girls passed the remaining books back and forth, flipping through pages of black and white drawings before settling on their choices. Megan claimed a collection of flowery bouquets, and Erin picked a medley of kaleido-scopic designs. Paige grabbed a book of big-winged birds.

Snatching up handfuls of crayons from the bucket, they began to color. The soft scratch of crayons moving across paper, the crackled rustle of turning pages, and the hum of the mini-fridge were the only sounds cutting into the silence of the subterranean room.

Suddenly, Paige dropped her crayon to the floor and leaned back against the couch, pressing her palm to her chest. "My heart..." She closed her eyes and swallowed. "It's racing."

So, like the good friend she was, Joanna jumped out of her seat and hurried over. Squatting at Paige's feet, she gripped her knees and looked up into her pale face. Tiny dots of sweat ringed the girl's upper lip, and a bluish vein in her neck pulsed. Joanna reached for her hands, enfolding them within her own. The feel of cold, clammy skin repulsed her, but Joanna kept her hands wrapped around Paige's.

"Paige, are you okay?" she asked, widening her eyes with feigned concern.

"I-I'm not sure." Paige blinked. "My heart's pounding, and I feel weird. Nervous kind of. Like something's wrong." She turned toward Erin and Megan who were both leaning back against the couch, their bodies limp, their coloring books abandoned. "What about you guys? Don't you feel weird?"

"I feel..." Megan giggled. "Good. Weird good, but good."

"Me too," Erin said, closing her eyes and arching her back.

"Then why am I...?" Paige's voice was a hoarse whisper. "Something's not right." She shook her head, and her chin trembled. Her eyes, glistening and damp, locked with Joanna's. "I'm scared."

"Paige, this is normal. Everybody reacts differently. Don't worry. I'm here." Keeping a hand on Paige's knee, Joanna got up from the floor and cocked her head toward Megan. "Let me sit next to her, Megan. Move over," she said.

Without opening her eyes, Megan slowly rolled her body away from Paige and dropped her head onto Erin's shoulder.

"Get off me," Erin grumbled, lifting her shoulder with a sharp jerk.

Megan exhaled in a loud, drawn-out sigh and tilted her

head back against the couch. "I'm hun-gry." Her words came out in a lazy drawl. "Any more brownies?"

"No, Megan. There are no more brownies," Joanna said. "Just relax."

She put a hand on Paige's shoulder, massaging it in gentle circles. "You okay?" She leaned toward her. "Paige?"

No response.

Cupping Paige's chin, Joanna turned the other girl's face toward her own. Her pupils were large and black, and her mouth was slightly open. Joanna touched her cheek. "Paige?"

Paige blinked, listlessly bobbing her head. "Huh?"

"Listen to me," Joanna said softly. "There's nothing for you to be afraid of. This happens to people sometimes. I'm here, and you're going to be fine." She patted Paige's knee. "Do you understand?"

Paige nodded and grasped Joanna's hand, lacing their fingers together.

Megan poked Joanna's thigh with her elbow. "What's wrong with Paige?"

"Paige?" Erin leaned forward, her eyes at half-mast. "What's the matter?" She tilted her head to the left and then to the right. "I feel good. Ve-ry good."

"Me too," Megan said, stretching her hands over her head. She reached for her coloring book, and leaning over Joanna, tossed it onto Paige's lap. "Look at this, Paige. Flowers. They'll make you feel better." She giggled. "So pretty."

Joanna glanced at the book laying open on Paige's lap. Crayoned slashes of purple, red, orange, and green ran roughshod over the outlined flowers.

Paige looked down at Megan's druggy art work, and her mouth dropped open. Her eyes grew wide. Backhanded, she flung the book onto the floor.

"What is that?" she yelled. "Those...those flowers...they weren't even flowers. They were...they were...I don't know what they were, but they were moving." She wrapped her arms around her chest.

"Paige, you're just dizzy. Nothing moved," Joanna said, opening a bottle of water and handing it to Paige. "Here. Drink this."

Paige took a deep swallow and leaned back against the couch.

"Do you trust me, Paige?" Joanna asked.

Paige lifted and lowered her head in a slow nod.

"Good. Then come with me." Joanna slipped her hand under Paige's arm and gently pulled her up. "I want you to lie down. You'll feel better."

Gripping Paige's elbow, Joanna led her to a pair of futons positioned along the far wall. Paige fell onto one of them, her body curling itself into a tight ball. Joanna perched on the neighboring futon and watched her. Paige closed her eyes, and her breathing deepened. Tiptoeing over to the built-in closet, Joanna pulled out a stack of pillows and comforters. Carefully, she slipped a pillow under Paige's head and covered her with a comforter.

She needs me. She trusts me. She's mine. The thoughts danced through Joanna's head. She carried a pair of pillows and comforters to the couch where Erin and Megan were lounging, their bodies limply draped like a pair of wet noodles.

"Guys, I need you to move so I can pull out the sofa bed."

"Huh?" Erin mumbled.

Megan stared, her face a blank. "What?"

"Up," Joanna said, waggling her fingers.

Stretching and groaning, Erin and Megan peeled themselves off the couch and stood. Joanna tossed the cushions onto the floor and pulled out the sofa bed, already fitted with a sheet, courtesy of her mother. She threw comforters and pillows at Erin and Megan, and they collapsed onto the bed. No changing into pajamas, no face washing, no tooth brushing.

Joanna climbed the two flights of stairs to her room. Opening her pajama drawer, she reached inside, then snatched her hand back. Better to stay in her clothes like the others. Still, she washed her face and brushed her teeth before heading back down to the basement.

Standing in the middle of the room, she did a final survey. Paige, Erin, and Megan—her three sleeping girls.

Settling into the futon next to Paige, Joanna closed her eyes.

Dawn caught sight of her watch as she opened the front door to her house and stepped inside. It was later than she had realized. A long dinner with Lisa coupled with heavier than usual traffic, and it was already almost midnight. She punched the code into the alarm keypad, silencing its soft beep. Hanging her jacket in the hall closet, she moved into the kitchen and snapped on the light.

Clean counters and not a single dirty dish in the sink. Such nice girls.

She headed down to the basement. The door was partway open, and she poked her head inside. A single lamp on a corner table glowed in the darkened room. She could make out the shapes of four sleeping girls, two on the sofa bed and two on futons. Someone's light snore was the only sound in the quiet room.

They must have had a hard day at the mall, Dawn thought, shaking her head and grinning. She'd wake up early and make them pancakes for breakfast. Buttermilk with chocolate chips.

Still smiling, she made her way back up the stairs.

8

Lowering herself into a squat, Grace gave Hendrix a quick two-handed neck massage and nuzzled her face against the top of his velvety head. His purr was a soft rumble like the hum of a refrigerator in a quiet room. "Be a good boy. I'll be back soon, okay?" she whispered and headed out the door.

Sinking into the porch swing, she tossed her crocheted shawl onto the cushioned seat and let the early fall air tickle her arms. The twilight sky was a streaky blend of orange, purple, and blue, and a cricket chorus had begun its evening serenade. She trained her eyes on the street and waited for Tom's silver BMW to round the corner.

"You make this old lady so happy," she would always whisper to Joanna after one of their regular family dinners.

"You're not an old lady, Grace-ma," would be Joanna's dependable reply.

But at sixty-seven, Grace had more years behind her than ahead.

If only she could re-live them...

She closed her eyes and shook her head. All those

years of worry, the way she read Dawn's diaries, snooped around her room, listened in on her conversations...Grace had invaded her daughter's privacy again and again and again.

Doug had never understood why Grace was so paranoid. That's what he had called her mothering style. "Paranoid." But the way he would tug on a lock of her hair and kiss her nose after he said it would make Grace laugh and shrug. Doug was the calm center of their little family solar system, and although Grace's path was a little wobbly at times, she and Dawn rotated happily around him.

Dawn grew up to be a beautiful, kind, and loving woman, and Grace had apologized and repaired their relationship a long time ago. These days it was a joy for her to watch her daughter be the kind of mother she wished she had been and to share with her and Tom the gift that was Joanna.

So, if she could do it all over again...

She would trust her child.

Tires crunched on the gravelly driveway, and Grace's eyes snapped open.

Climbing into the backseat of Tom's car, she settled in next to Joanna.

~

Stepping under the red awing hanging over the restaurant's door, Grace, Dawn, and Joanna followed Tom into *Tony's*.

"Hi, Gina." Tom waved at the dark-haired girl perched on a high stool behind the cash register, her thumbs flying across her cell phone.

Gina looked up. "Hey, Mr. Harvey. Hey, guys." She smiled and pointed toward the back of the restaurant. "Your table's ready. I'll tell my dad you're here," she said, jumping off her stool.

"Don't bother him. Give the guy a rest." Tom laughed. "And you can go back to texting."

Her face flushed, and she giggled.

Tom, his family in tow, walked past the brick-walled pizza oven and claimed their usual table.

Tony, *the* Tony of *Tony's*, bounded out of the kitchen, his belly leading the way, and trotted over to the table. Placing a big hand on Tom's shoulder, he nodded at Grace, Dawn, and Joanna, smiling at each of them in turn.

"Ladies," he said, then turning to Tom. "So, where've you been, Tommy boy? I missed you last week."

Tom lifted his palms in surrender. "Business, Tony. You know how it is."

"Yeah, yeah, I do." Tony clapped his hands together. "So, the usual?"

"The usual," Tom said.

"The usual" was a crusty loaf of garlic bread, a Caesar salad, and the best spaghetti and meatballs any of them had ever tasted, all served family style.

"Almost as good as yours, Dawn," Tom said between bites, winking at his wife.

Dawn rolled her eyes and laughed.

Joanna kicked her grandmother under the table. In answer, Grace squeezed her thigh.

The food wasn't the only, or even the primary, reason Tom loved *Tony's*. A child of jet-setting parents, he had grown up in a luxury Manhattan duplex under the care of a succession of nannies. Regular patronage at a *Cheers* sort of bar or restaurant "where everybody knows your name" might have been a reality for other people, but for Tom, it had been a dream. And Dawn's decision to leave a successful career in business and move to the suburbs as a full-time mother to Joanna had been *her* choice and *her* dream.

"Tell us about Shanghai, Tom," Grace said, turning to look at her son-in-law.

Tom answered with a quick summation of his trip. Presentations for dark-suited executives in wood-paneled conference rooms, too-long dinners in overpriced restaurants billed to a corporate client, and hours spent alone in an amenities-stocked hotel room prepping for the next day's meetings. One more business trip to one more foreign city that he didn't have the time to enjoy or the energy to explore. In other words, it was the same old, same old. And like always, Tom seemed more interested in hearing about the everyday goings-on in the life of his family than in talking about his own.

Lifting a forkful of spaghetti, he leaned toward his daughter. "So, what did I miss in Joanna-land this week?"

"Nothing special, Dad," Joanna said. "I went to school, did my homework, went to the mall, had a sleepover." She shrugged. "That's it."

"That's it?" Tom raised an eyebrow, clearly wanting more. "I've been away for a week. Your mom tells me more about what goes on in a single day than that."

Tilting her head, Dawn pulled her face into an exaggerated pout and elbowed Tom. He faked a grimace, and they both laughed.

Tom was a good match for Dawn, Grace thought, just as Doug had been for her. And although Grace knew Tom would be just as happy if instead of developing strategies for mega-companies, he had taken over Doug's hardware store in town and eaten dinner with his family every night, that was never his life's path.

Tom turned to Grace. "And what about you, Grace? What've you been doing?"

He caught her with her mouth full. Holding up a finger, she finished chewing and swallowed.

"Just the usual. Yoga class, book group, helping out at the library."

"What are you doing there these days?" he asked.

"Homework help, story time, sorting through donations for the book sale. They're so understaffed. I do whatever they need me to." Grace stopped and pointed first at Dawn, then at Joanna. "And these two volunteer there also."

"I like to read to the kids and do arts and crafts sometimes," Dawn said.

"And Joanna's specialty," Grace said, tapping her granddaughter's shoulder, "is sorting through the used books and CDs that people donate."

"Hardcovers for two dollars, trade paperbacks and CDs for a dollar, and mass markets for fifty cents," Joanna spouted off the price list. "And I'm a customer as well as a sorter. That's how I got *Stranger in a Strange Land* and my Santana CD."

"A double contributor." Dawn laughed.

"Actually, I would have been a triple contributor. There was a Beatles CD that I wanted to get for Grace-ma, but—"

"Oh no!" Dawn cut in. "No Beatles for your grandmother. She can't stand them."

"I found that out." Joanna said. "They're the one band from the Sixties that Grace-ma *doesn't* like."

Three heads swiveled toward Grace.

Her body stiffened, and she shifted in her chair, bringing her hands together in a tight clasp below the table.

"I just never got into their music," she said. "I don't know why." She tilted her head and lifted a corner of her mouth, shaping her face into an expression consistent with her words. "I really don't," she said and plunged her fork into her last remaining meatball.

"Well, Beatles or not, I'm proud of you," Tom said, pushing his empty plate away. "All of you." His eyes moved from Grace to Dawn to Joanna.

"It's no big deal." Joanna shrugged.

Tom lifted his chin and winked. "Well, it is to me."

Dawn patted Tom's arm and pulled her cell phone from her bag. "So, what is your schedule like over the next few weeks, Mr. Captain of Industry?" She laughed. "You rattled off some dates to me before, but I need to put them in my phone."

"The usual late nights at the office, a couple of client meetings, and I need to be away again next month."

Dawn looked up from her phone. "Where to this time?"

"Los Angeles. I have a one-day conference." Tom reached for his water glass and took a long sip. "But *we'll* be gone for a week." He waggled his eyebrows, keeping his mouth neutral.

"*We?*" Dawn asked.

"What do you think about spending a week out there with me?"

"Just the two of us?" Dawn's eyebrows shot up.

"Just the two of us," Tom said.

"You'll take the week off?"

Tom crossed his arms over his chest and nodded like a genie granting a wish. "I'll take the week off."

Dawn slapped a hand down on her knee, her eyes wide. "I'm in," she yelped. "But wait." Her head turned toward Joanna and then swiveled back to Tom. "What about Joanna? She can't stay alone."

"I can––" Grace jumped in.

"Grace-ma can stay with me," Joanna finished her grandmother's thought.

"That's what I was hoping." Tom smiled and turned to his wife, "Dawn?"

"I don't know, Tom. That's a lot for my mother––"

"No, it's not. Joanna's my buddy." Grace slung her arm around her granddaughter and hugged her. "I've stayed with her before when you've been away. Quite a few times."

Joanna moved closer to Grace. "That's true."

"Those were for *weekend* trips, not whole weeks," Dawn said.

"It would just be for one week. Not *weeks*," Joanna placed her hands on the table, her eyes on Dawn. "And it would give us some time together to work on the scrapbook." She turned toward Grace. "Right, Grace-ma?"

"Yes, definitely." Grace lowered her head in a sharp nod, holding back a smile.

Dawn looked from Joanna to Grace. "I'm not sure about this, Mom. A week is a long time for you to––"

Grace, knowing that the battle had already been won, reached across the table to pat her daughter's hand. "Dawn, go away with your husband. Joanna and I will be fine."

Dawn breathed in and then out. Pushing her lips together, her mouth curved upward, and she nodded slowly.

"You *all* make this old lady so happy," Grace said.

"Grace-ma, you're not––" Joanna began.

"Old!" Tom and Dawn yelled in a happy chorus.

H oisting her backpack over her shoulder, Joanna raced to the front door. "Bye, Mom," she called, slamming the door behind her.

The big yellow bus had just made its wide angle turn onto her street and was lumbering toward her house. Joanna ran down the lawn, reaching the sidewalk just as the bus shuddered to a stop.

"Well, at least I didn't have to wait for you today." The bus driver shot her his standard squint-eyed glare.

"Sorry, Mr. Ferguson," Joanna said in her sweet-little-girl voice.

The driver shook his head and chuckled. Joanna climbed onto the bus and moving past the familiar group-ings of other high school students still too young to drive, dropped her backpack onto the last seat and plopped down next to it.

Pulling out *Stranger in a Strange Land,* she leaned back against the window and stretched her legs across the seat. She had ten minutes and two more stops to read until the doors would fly open, spitting its passengers out in front of Oakdale High School.

The bus made its first stop, then its second, and more seats were filled. Joanna reached her arm out to the seat in front of her, bracing herself for the familiar sharp right turn onto Main Street. But instead, the bus continued straight on Northridge Avenue. The hubbub of voices around her suddenly morphed into a low buzz, and as if by prearranged signal, the entire busload of school-bound passengers turned toward the windows.

A few rows in front of Joanna, a dark-haired boy leaned into the aisle and cupped his hands around his mouth. "Where are we going, Fergie?" he yelled.

"New student. Settle down, folks," came the bellowed response.

A new student? In mid-October? It seemed kind of weird, but what did Joanna care?

The early morning school bus conversations went back to their usual just-below-a-roar volume, and she returned to her book. A few more minutes on Northridge, and the bus turned right. Joanna glanced up at the small green and white street sign. Evergreen Lane. She'd never heard of it.

The road narrowed, and the bus slowed. The houses were spaced widely apart and set back from the street. Up until then, all the stops had been in housing developments stocked with newish homes sporting well-kept lawns and two- or three-car garages. Evergreen Lane didn't even have sidewalks.

"Are we still in Oakdale?" someone called out.

A girl sitting toward the front of the bus turned around. "Yeah, we are, but this is *old money* Oakdale. Kids who live back here all go to private school," she announced.

"Calm down, guys. Next person who says something

disrespectful...I'll write you up," Mr. Ferguson barked, keeping his eyes trained on the road. "And I mean it."

The cacophony of voices ratcheted down to a muted babble, and Mr. Ferguson drove on. Joanna stared out the window and counted mailboxes––one, two, three––each marking a long driveway leading up to a large house half-hidden behind a thick grove of leafy trees. At the fourth mailbox, a tall, slim girl looked up from her phone, and the bus came to a stop.

Even from her seat at the back, Joanna could see that the white-blonde color of the hair grazing the girl's shoulders had been created by a cutting-edge stylist. No one local, not even at her mother's overpriced salon, could create something like that. A black beret tilted back on the girl's head and dark sunglasses completed her look.

The new girl climbed onto the bus and waved her hand in a wide arc. "Hi all, I'm Quinn," she said and marched, black lace-up boots thumping, to the back of the bus, parking herself in the empty seat in front of Joanna.

Slipping her book into her backpack, Joanna turned in her seat and stared at the emerald lawn landscape sliding past her window.

Who was this freak?

Two more stops, and the bus pulled up to the school. Kids gathered their books, bags, and backpacks, jamming the narrow center aisle as they pushed their way up to the open door. Quinn waited for the crowd to pass, and Joanna watched her slither out of her seat before leaving her own. She flipped her white hair over her black shirt and stepped between the parallel rows of now empty seats, slowly making her way to the front of the bus.

"Thanks, mister." She flashed Fergie a wide grin. Lifting

her hand in a wave, or maybe it was a salute, she jumped off the bus.

Her nails were bitten to the quick.

Once inside the building, Quinn split off from the mass of students heading to the locker hallway and ducked into the principal's office. New student paperwork? Whatever...

Joanna hated to be stuck in the middle of the herd. So, with a strategically positioned right shoulder and a few mumbled "excuse me"s, she made her way to her locker. Paige, Erin, and Megan leaned against the wall, waiting.

"Your bus late today?" Paige asked.

"A little," Joanna said. "Had to pick up a new girl."

"Now? That's weird," Erin said cocking her head. "School just started a few weeks ago. Why didn't she come then?"

Joanna shrugged and dialed the combination to her locker. Stashing her backpack inside, she grabbed the books she needed for first and second periods. The warning bell rang, and the girls separated, scrambling down the hall and darting into their individual homerooms. Fifteen minutes later they were on their way to their first period classes.

Joanna took her usual seat in the last row of Mr. Reed's honors geometry class. She did her homework and kept up her A+ average, and he let her chew gum. That was their unspoken agreement. Hey, it worked.

Paige slipped into the seat next to Joanna, and propping her elbow on the desk, leaned toward her. "Mr. Reed looks especially hot today, doesn't he?" She licked her lips without showing her braces. "Too bad for Erin and Megan they can't be in the honors class, huh?"

Paige was right. Tim Reed, their just-out-of-college geometry teacher with rock hard arms and longish hair that was the kind of sun-streaked that couldn't be bought, was hot. H-O-T. Hot. Every girl in Oakdale High School knew it, and Joanna was sure Timmy Boy did too. And to be honest, she had thought about...well...never mind. Joanna could ace his class easily enough on her own. Plus, getting involved with a teacher was stupid. And "stupid" was one thing Joanna definitely was not.

"Calm down, Paige," Joanna said, rolling her eyes.

The rest of the class trickled in, scraping back chairs, dropping books, and digging for pencils.

Mr. Reed closed the door and scooped up the pile of stapled sheets stacked in the center of his desk. "Okay folks, it's test day. Books away. Desks clear. You'll have the whole period to––"

Suddenly the door swung open with a loud whoosh, and Quinn burst into the room.

"Mr. Reed?" She said his name as a question, not waiting for an answer. "I'm Quinn Chandler. I'm supposed to be in this class."

"Yes, I was told that you'd be coming today, Quinn. But I'm about to hand out a test. So, if you'd like to grab a seat and do some other work..." He pointed to an empty desk at the front of the room.

"Thanks, but I can take the test." She strode over to the desk. "I don't mind."

"No, that's not necessary. It's your first day. We'll talk about catching you up later."

"It's okay. I'm ready," she said, raising her chin and meeting Mr. Reed's eyes.

"I don't think that would be fair to you, Quinn." He shook his head. "Not on your first day."

"I'll take my chances," she said, squaring her shoulders and clasping her hands behind her back.

Joanna sat up in her seat. Was that a challenge? A dare? The room grew quiet.

Mr. Reed clicked his tongue. "No problem," he said. Looking down at the stack of tests in his hands, he counted out a pile and handed it to the first person in the row closest to the door. "Pass them back, please." He repeated the process for each of the next four rows, handing the last pile to Quinn. "Good luck," he said, tossing his words into the center of the room.

Joanna wrote her name at the top of the first page and set out to prove that line segment AB equaled line segment CD.

She finished the test ten minutes before the end of the period and glanced over at Quinn. The new girl's pencil lay across her paper, and her head was turned toward the window.

Was she done already?

The room was warm, but a cold shiver prickled the back of Joanna's neck.

Mr. Reed collected the tests, and the end-of-class bell rang. Joanna jumped out of her seat and scooped up her books and notebooks. Still in her chair, Paige's head swiveled in Quinn's direction. Joanna followed her gaze.

Quinn leaned back in her chair, stretched, and yawned. Picking up her single notebook, she stood. She arched her back and yawned again. Then, tapping the notebook against her thigh, and tilting her head back, she pivoted and scanned the room.

Joanna looked down at Paige. "What are you doing? Let's go."

Paige gathered up her books and followed Joanna to the door and out of the classroom. In the crowded hall, they joined the swarm of students rushing to their second period classes.

"So, what do you think of the new girl?" Paige asked, leaning so close to Joanna that their shoulders grazed.

"Weird hair," Joanna muttered and continued walking.

"Why do you think she took the test? She didn't have to," Paige said, keeping pace with Joanna. "It doesn't make sense." She touched Joanna's elbow. "Does it?"

"Don't know." Joanna shrugged. "Don't care."

"I-I don't care either," Paige said quickly. "Just curious. That's all."

Joanna flipped her hair over her shoulder. "I'm not," she said. "Anyway, see you at lunch." Turning left, she headed for second period U.S. history.

Erin and Megan had already claimed their usual seats at the back of the room, leaving a desk for Joanna between them.

"Hey, guys," Joanna said, dropping her books and pulling out her chair.

"Hey, Joanna," their voices chimed out in unison, but their eyes were focused on the door.

With a sharp swivel of her head, Joanna turned to follow their gaze.

Quinn swooped into the room, a white sheet of paper dangling from her hand, and strutted over to Mrs. Bergstrom's desk. Mrs. B. looked up, and Quinn handed her the paper.

Joanna felt her jaw clench and her nostrils flare. Not here too.

"You may take any seat you like," Mrs. B. said, pointing

into the classroom and waving her finger in an arc through the air. "And Quinn..." She cleared her throat. "Please remove your hat. I don't allow that sort of thing in the classroom."

Quinn clamped her lips together into a tight line. She pulled off her beret and shook out her hair. "No problem," she said and stalked off to an empty desk in the corner of the room.

"That girl is fierce." Erin's words flew out of her mouth in a loud hiss.

"She was in my homeroom this morning," Megan said. "I don't think she's from around here."

"She sure doesn't look like it. And she doesn't act like it either." Erin pulled her lower lip into her mouth and shook her head.

"Well, she lives here now," Joanna said. "She was on my bus this morning."

"*That* was the new girl on your bus?" Megan asked.

"Uh-huh." Joanna nodded.

Erin squinted and leaned toward Joanna. "Where does she live?"

"Out in the middle of nowhere."

"Students, quiet please." Mrs. B.'s booming voice stopped their conversation. "We have a lot to do today, and I'd like to get started. We'll be having the unit test on the thirteen colonies at the end of the week, and I thought we'd review a little differently this time. So, first of all, I'd like everyone to please stand." She lifted her hands in a single swift motion.

A chorus of groans accompanied the raspy creak of the room's metal chairs being pushed back.

Ignoring the sound effects, Mrs. B. pushed a stray curl of gray hair behind her ear. "Good. Now, please line up around the perimeter of the room."

With elaborately drawn-out sighs and exaggerated eye rolls, the students followed her instructions.

"Okay, I've got a series of questions here." Mrs. B. grabbed a stack of index cards from her desk. "One by one, I'll ask you to answer them. If and when you get your question wrong, please return to your seat. At the end, whoever is left standing will earn ten points added on to his or her test score."

"Amy," Mrs. B. said, pointing to the first girl in line. "Which of the thirteen colonies was founded by religious dissenters?"

The girl rubbed her chin. "Um, Massachusetts?"

Mrs. B. shook her head and placed the index card on her desk. "I'm sorry, Amy. The answer is Rhode Island. Please take your seat."

The stack of cards in Mrs. B.'s hands dwindled as did the number of students still standing until only Quinn, a short, red-faced boy named Seth, and Joanna remained. Seth didn't know that the state with the largest number of signers of the Declaration of Independence was Pennsylvania, and Mrs. B. asked him to return to his seat.

It was down to Joanna and Quinn.

"What was the predominant church in the colonial South?" Mrs. B. looked at Joanna.

"The Church of England," Joanna answered.

"Georgia was founded for a certain group of people. Who were they?" Mrs. B. asked Quinn.

"Debtors," Quinn said.

"What boundary separated the middle colonies from the southern colonies?"

"The Mason-Dixon line," Joanna responded.

"Two of the three major crops of the Carolinas were rice and tobacco. What was the third?"

"Indigo." Quinn smiled.

"Who founded the colony of––"

The end-of-class bell rang, and the seated students pushed back their chairs and reached for their papers and books.

Mrs. B. held up a finger and announced to the class. "Well, it seems like we have a tie between Joanna and our new student, Quinn." She pivoted and faced the two girls. "So, I'll split the prize, and each of you will have five points added to your test score." Turning back to the class, she clapped loudly, and a handful of students joined her. "Please remember to read and outline chapter seven for tomorrow," she called out.

With a mumbled "thank you" to Mrs. B., Joanna turned away from Quinn and returned to her desk where Erin and Megan had already stacked her books.

"Congratulations, Joanna. I can't believe you knew all those answers." Megan squeezed Joanna's arm.

"It wasn't a big deal," Joanna said. "Anyway, Quinn knew them too," she added.

Better to deal with the elephant in the room now rather than later.

"Yeah, how did that happen? This is her first day in the class," Erin said.

Megan jabbed her knee into Erin's.

Joanna pretended not to notice and shrugged her shoulders, turning toward the door. "It happens," she said. "Anyway, I need to stop at my locker before gym class. See you guys at lunch." Snatching up her books, she bolted out of the classroom.

～

Joanna's gym elective for the marking period was yoga. And after the debacle that was history class, she was especially ready for some "perfect tranquility." Changing into shorts and a t-shirt, she grabbed a mat from her locker and headed into the gym.

As usual, the class began with breathing. Abdomen, diaphragm, and chest. Then it was on to Child's Pose. Joanna rested her forehead on her mat and extended her arms behind her body, palms up. She breathed, and her body followed the familiar sequence. Downward-Facing Dog, Cobra, Cow, Cat, Sphinx, Cat, Cow, Cobra, Downward-Facing Dog, and Child's Pose. The series ended with the Corpse pose.

"This is not nap time," the teacher reminded the class.

Joanna lay on her back, legs and arms apart, and relaxed. Or tried to. But after just a few minutes, she accepted the fact that "perfect tranquility" or any sort of tranquility was simply not reachable for her. Not today anyway.

Joanna strolled into the cafeteria and over to her regular table. Four of the six seats had already been claimed, marked with scattered books strategically positioned across the laminate table and matching chairs that were supposed to look like wood.

Erin, Megan, and Paige had done their jobs.

Joanna added her own books to their arrangement and headed over to the serving line. Megan spotted her and waved her over, pointing to the extra tray she had been pushing along the railing. A tall girl with frizzy blonde hair and an angry red pimple on her chin narrowed her eyes and stared as Joanna passed her, but no one else on the line seemed to care.

"Thanks, guys," Joanna said, wedging herself between Megan and Erin and leaning over to wave at Paige who was up ahead.

Joanna opted for her usual minestrone soup and vegetable wrap. Erin got a chicken fajita, and Paige ordered a chef salad with yogurt dressing. Megan went for her usual too—a hamburger, fries, and chocolate milk. At the table, the girls slid their books into one corner, settled into their seats, and began to eat.

Fixing her eyes on Joanna, Paige dug a fork into her salad. "So, Erin and Megan told me what happened in history. You know...with the new girl."

Paige. It was always Paige. What was it with her?

Joanna had thought that by serving Paige a *special* brownie and then taking her under her wing like a mother hen, she would have gotten her to settle down a bit and appreciate her place in the pecking order—side by side with Erin and Megan, and *below* Joanna. Paige should have been thankful to Joanna for taking care of her at the sleepover. But no, instead, she kept trying to get under her skin. Maybe she still didn't accept the fact that Joanna was smarter than she was. But no matter how hard Paige tried to get her to lose control, that was *not* going to happen.

Joanna kept her face neutral. "Yeah?" she said, raising her eyebrows.

"Well, it *is* odd. Isn't it?" Paige said, her question a challenge. "It's her first day here and..." Her eyes darted to a spot behind Joanna's head, and her voice trailed off.

Joanna felt a pair of hands grip and then squeeze her shoulders. She leaned back and looked up, although she didn't have to. She knew who it was.

"Hey," Ryan said, his clear gray eyes locking with hers.

"Hey," Joanna echoed his favorite word and shaped her lips into a close-mouthed smile.

Pulling out the empty chair next to her, Ryan lowered his long lean body into it. "I missed you Saturday night," he said, cocking his head and tapping her knee.

Joanna turned her body sideways in her chair, crossed her legs, and ran a hand through her hair. "Yeah?"

"Yeah." Ryan grinned.

Opening her eyes wide, Joanna continued the flirtation dance. "Next time?"

"Next time." He touched her nose and stood. Turning to the others, he waved and slowly walked back to his own table.

Uncrossing her legs, Joanna swiveled her body back and faced her girls. Paige and Erin were silent, their lips slightly parted. Megan lifted a fry to her mouth.

They could all learn from her, and they knew it. But it wasn't only about technique. Joanna was well aware that through no doing of her own, she was lucky enough to have been born with the kind of looks guys liked. Long dark hair, the kind that didn't frizz even if she didn't blow dry it, and a slim yet curvy body. But even more than that, it was her eyes that did it. No one in her family knew where their dark brown color had come from. Must have been from someone way back on her dad's side. Anyway, she'd been told, and she knew, that they were mesmerizing. Hard to look away from. Powerful.

Also, she was very, very smart. And she knew that too.

But Joanna didn't deceive herself. She knew she wasn't all that unusual. Like everyone else, she'd been born with certain gifts. Certain talents. The crucial difference was that *she* had learned how to use them.

She turned to Paige. "So, what is it that you were saying about the new girl? Quinn? Is that her name?"

"Nothing. I was just wondering..."

Joanna leaned back in her chair and, sliding her hips forward, stretched her legs out under the table. "Yeah?"

"Never mind." Paige licked her lips and looked down at her salad. "It wasn't important," she mumbled.

Joanna glanced at Erin, her mouth full of fajita, and then at Megan, who was noisily slurping her chocolate milk through a straw. She shrugged and bit into her wrap.

10

"I'll make sure the house is stocked with food, Mom. And you won't have to do much driving because Joanna takes the bus to school. If you want to, you can even--"

"Dawn, please. Stop." Grace laughed into the phone, interrupting her daughter's monologue. "I'm perfectly capable of buying food, driving, and taking care of anything else that needs to be done while you're away," she said. "Please don't worry. Everything will be fine."

"I know it will. I'm not worried. It's just that I think--"

"I know what you think, Dawn. You think it's a lot for me, but it's really--"

"You're right," she said. "I do think it's a lot for you. And besides that, I don't want to take advantage of you. You're busy. You have your own life."

Grace shook her head and smiled. Too bad Dawn couldn't see her face. Then she'd understand. She pressed the phone to her ear and tried to explain.

"Dawn, this is not a favor. Having me spend the week with Joanna, just the two of us, is a gift that you and Tom are giving me. All of you are the most important people in my life. You know that. And Joanna? She's such a special girl. I'm truly touched..." Grace's voice cracked, and her eyes watered. "I'm touched that she wants to spend time with her old Grace-ma."

"Mom, you're—"

"I know. I know." Grace chuckled. "I. Am. Not. Old."

"Now you got it." Dawn laughed. "But what about Hendrix? I didn't even think about him. Uh...what if you brought him here? I'd have to ask Tom, of course. His allergies...but maybe if you could keep him out of our bedroom, and if we vacuumed really well—"

"Don't worry about Hendrix, Dawn. He's a cat. I'll be with him at my house while Joanna's at school, and I'll take her back with me to visit him if she has time. He'll just be alone at night. It's not a problem," Grace said. "Really."

"Mom, are you sure you want to do this? A hundred percent sure? It's not just for a weekend this time. We'll be gone for a whole week. Why don't you think about it? You don't have to let me know now."

"I don't need to think about it, Dawn. Let me do this," Grace said. "Please."

11

Q uinn was on Joanna's bus, in her geometry class, and in her history class. And then suddenly, she appeared at Joanna's lunch table. Something about a schedule change. Quinn had been moved into a higher level French which meant a transfer into Paige's bio class and a lunch period switch. And of course, Paige was the one who had waved her over to their table. Without asking anyone. Without asking Joanna.

So now, sitting diagonally across from Joanna, wearing her stupid beret on her stupid bleached-white hair, was Quinn Chandler.

Paige leaned toward her. "So, you left a private school in Manhattan to come *here*? To Oakdale?" she asked, her elbows on the table, chin resting on her folded hands. "Why?"

"Why not? I live here." Quinn shrugged, her head swiveling from Paige to Megan and then down to Megan's tray. "Can I have a couple of those?" She pointed to the mound of fries on Megan's plate.

Megan's head bobbed in an open-mouthed nod, and Quinn reached across the table and snatched up a fistful of fries. Megan stared as one by one, Quinn devoured the fries and licked the salt from her fingertips.

Joanna knew what Megan was thinking. Quinn was the kind of girl who could eat whatever she wanted without gaining weight. Good genes. Joanna had them too. But Quinn was tall which was another advantage in Megan's doomed-to-be-chubby world.

A wave of heat crept up Joanna's body, and her scalp prickled. Luckily, she didn't have the kind of skin that turned red, which was an emotional giveaway. More good genes. They must have been the throwback kind because they certainly hadn't come from her fair-skinned parents or grandparents. She should probably be thankful to some unknown someone up in her family tree.

Joanna was careful to keep her expression neutral, unsurprised. She hadn't known Quinn had gone to a private school in the city. How did Paige find that out? They must have been getting chummy in bio class. But Quinn hadn't answered Paige's question. Why *had* she come here? And that led Joanna to another question...

"Why'd you start here in October though instead of the beginning of the year?" she asked, keeping her voice even. Casual. She bit into her wrap and chewed.

Quinn reached for her water bottle and took a long gulp. "I finally convinced my parents to let me transfer over."

"That's too bad," Erin said quietly. "It would have been easier for you if you could have started back in September along with everyone else."

"I guess," Quinn said, flipping her hair over her shoulder. "But I'm here now."

And so was Ryan. Joanna heard his footsteps coming up

behind her. He tapped her on the shoulder and slid into the chair next to her, his hand grazing her knee.

"Hey, girls," he said, scanning the table, his eyes stopping at Quinn. "I'm Ryan," he said. To *her*.

"I'm Quinn." She smiled and lifted her hand in greeting.

"You new here?"

She nodded. "Second day."

"So, what do you think so far?"

"I don't know." Quinn shrugged. "Too early to tell."

"Where'd you move from?"

"I didn't move. I live in Oakdale, but I used to go to a private school," Quinn said. "In the city," she added, squaring her shoulders and tossing her head back.

"Cool." Ryan nodded. "Well, hope you like it here." He stood and ran a finger down Joanna's arm, his eyes still on Quinn. "See you, girls," he said and ambled back to his own table.

Erin opened her mouth, then closed it. Paige's lips came together in a pursed grin, and Megan reached for the last fry on her plate. Quinn adjusted her beret and leaned back in her chair, her face a blank. Unreadable.

None of Joanna's girls were in her Spanish class. Neither was Quinn. That was good. Joanna needed the break. She slunk back in her seat next to the open window, letting the not-too-cool, not-too-warm breeze that only came in the fall tickle her arm. Turning to the front of the room, she forced herself to look at the teacher.

"Today I'd like to go over the most common irregular verb conjugations," Señora Lopez announced. She began with *querer*. To want.

Yo quiero, tu quieres, el quiere, nosotros queremos, vosotros queries, ellos quieren.

I want, you want, he wants, we want, you (plural) want, they want.

And yes, Joanna did want.

She wanted Quinn to go back to wherever the hell it was that she came from.

12

The school bus rumbled as it turned onto the street. When she could, Dawn liked to be home when Joanna arrived just in case she'd be in the mood to talk. Helicopter parenting wasn't her style, and luckily, her daughter wasn't the kind of kid she needed to worry about. Thank goodness! She'd heard so many stories...drugs, alcohol, promiscuous sex, you name it.

The fact that Joanna valued her privacy didn't disturb her. At her daughter's age, Dawn had valued hers too, but... well, that was water under the bridge. Anyway, sometimes Joanna did let her in--a little bit. And when that mood did strike her, Dawn was always ready and waiting.

The front door opened and closed with a louder than usual bang.

"I'm in the kitchen, hon," Dawn called out, wiping her hands on a towel.

"--kay," Joanna answered, her voice a low-pitched grumble.

Uh-oh. Dawn tossed the towel onto the counter and stepped into the foyer. Joanna was already at the hall closet, sliding her jacket onto a hanger. Turning slowly, she faced her mother, her lips curved into an artificial smile.

"Hi," she said quietly.

"Hungry?"

Joanna shrugged and followed Dawn into the kitchen.

"What would you like? Fruit? Hummus dip? A granola bar? Trail mix?"

"Nah, never mind. I guess I'm not really hungry." Joanna shook her head and turned to leave.

"How about hot chocolate? It's that kind of day, isn't it?" Dawn peered out the window over the sink. The sky was a streaky collage of gray, blue, and pink, and the lawn was dotted with red and gold leaves.

"Hmm...Yeah, maybe I'll have some hot chocolate." Joanna moved to stand next to her mother, their shoulders touching, and shared her view of the late afternoon sky.

Dawn patted her daughter's arm. "Go sit down. I'll get it ready."

Joanna gathered spoons and napkins, and Dawn poured milk into two mugs and slid them into the microwave. Stirring in a couple of tablespoons of cocoa mix, she topped their drinks with mini-marshmallows and carried them to the table. Joanna smiled, a real one this time, and dipped her spoon into her mug, leaning down to blow on the steaming hot chocolate.

"So, how was school today?" Dawn asked.

"Meh," Joanna answered without looking up.

"Meh?"

"Just the usual." Joanna slurped a spoonful of hot chocolate. "There's a new girl in a couple of my classes. She came yesterday."

"In October?"

"Uh-huh."

"That's odd. It's so close to the beginning of the school year. Too bad her parents couldn't have moved here earlier." Dawn sipped her drink.

"They didn't actually *move* here. They already lived in Oakdale."

"And she started school *now*? In October? Where did she—?"

"She...*Quinn*...that's her name..." Joanna rolled her eyes. "She came from a private school. In New York."

"That's odd. Do you know where she lives?"

"Yeah, she lives off Northridge. Evergreen Lane." Joanna scooped up a marshmallow with her spoon and popped it into her mouth.

"Evergreen Lane?"

"Uh-huh. She's on my bus."

Dawn drummed fingers along the edge of the table. "What's her last name?"

"Chandler." Joanna tilted her head, her eyes narrowing into a squint. "Why?"

Dawn looked down into her cup and slowly swirled her spoon in lazy circles through her cocoa.

Chandler...Chandler... It sounded familiar.

And then, she remembered.

She brought the mug to her lips and drank, letting the chocolatey warmth flow down her throat and spread through her chest. "No reason. Just wanted to see if I knew the family," she said and dabbed her mouth with her napkin. "But I don't."

"Doesn't matter." Joanna shrugged and stood, arching her back in a wide stretch. "Anyway, I've got homework." She carried her cup to the sink and turned the water on.

∾

Who was Quinn Chandler? And why was she at Oakdale High?

If Joanna just knew the *who*, maybe she could figure out the *why*. But even her mom, who seemed to know everyone in town, didn't know Quinn or her family. Although why would she? The Chandlers didn't live in one of the typical-for-Oakdale developments that seemed to spawn stay-at-home moms who belonged to the PTA and did volunteer work.

No, the Chandlers lived in a house shielded by a long, long driveway and a heavy thicket of trees. Joanna knew that kind of privacy must have cost some serious money. *That* Oakdale was a world away from her own, and it was a world away from that of every other student enrolled in the town's only high school.

So, why was Quinn here? Had she specifically wanted to transfer into Oakdale High? Or had it been more about *getting out* of some posh private school in the city?

Quinn could tell any story she wanted, but there was one surefire way for Joanna to find out what she needed to know. She flopped onto her bed and reached for her laptop.

Quinn Chandler.

She googled the new girl's name.

Nothing.

She searched Facebook, Twitter, Instagram, Snapchat, and Pinterest.

Still nothing.

She tried three other search engines, but all that came up was a football player in Idaho and a singer in South Carolina. Not her girl. She searched *Chandler*, *Chandler Evergreen Lane*, and *Chandler Oakdale New Jersey* and still, she learned only the basics about a Chandler family in Oakdale.

Richard and Tonya Chandler had two children. Derek

and Elizabeth, no ages given. Richard was in "agribusiness," and they lived in a big house situated on a large piece of land on Evergreen Lane. But there was no mention of Quinn.

And none of them were on social media.

handler.

It had taken Dawn a moment to place the name, but then she remembered. The girl from Oakdale who'd been expelled from the Tinsley Academy. Something about an affair with a teacher and then a car fire. Lisa had told her about it a few weeks earlier. Her daughter was a student at Tinsley.

But *Quinn*? An odd name. Not one that Dawn would have forgotten. She lifted her landline phone from its cradle and carried it into the living room. Sinking into the soft leather couch, she punched in Lisa's number.

"Hi, Dawn," Lisa answered on the second ring.

"Glad I caught you. You busy?"

"Nope. Done with my last sales call, Chloe's at soccer practice, and Alex is working on a social studies project with his friends. Or he better be." She laughed. "Ken's still at the hospital. Emergency C-section. So, I'm all yours, babe."

"Good. I have a question for you," Dawn said. "Remember the story you told me about the girl at Chloe's school? The one who had an affair with a teacher and set fire to his car?"

"Of course, I do. People are still talking about it. But the girl wasn't the one who had the affair. It was her mother."

"Her mother? Really? I don't remember that part. Can you tell me the story again?"

"Sure. But why?"

"Was the girl's last name 'Chandler'?"

"Yes, Elizabeth Chandler. Why? What's going on?"" Lisa asked, her words fired out in a quick staccato.

"Aah." Dawn slipped a throw pillow behind her head and leaned back. "Luckily, nothing. There's a new girl in a few of Joanna's classes. She transferred from a Manhattan private school, and I recognized the name 'Chandler' from the story you told me. But this girl's first name is 'Quinn', not 'Elizabeth'."

The line went quiet.

"Lisa? You there?"

Lisa's loud tongue click was followed by a long exhale. "Dawn?"

"Yeah?" Dawn said, her body tensing.

"Elizabeth Chandler always went by 'Quinn'. That's her middle name."

Dawn's mouth filled with the taste of metal. She swallowed and cleared her throat, but the taste was still there. "Lisa, tell me what happened. I need to know the whole story," she said, her voice scratchy and thin.

Ten minutes later Dawn said good-bye to Lisa and called Tom.

"You have reached..."

She hung up without leaving a message. Tom was at work, and the situation was too complicated to explain in a voicemail. Besides, it wasn't an emergency, and hopefully, it never would be. Still, now that she knew who Quinn Chandler was, Dawn had a decision to make. And besides Tom, there was only one other person in the world who loved Joanna as much as she did.

She dialed her mother's number.

"So, a fourteen-year-old girl walks in on her mother in bed with one of her teachers and sets fire to the teacher's car? And now that girl is in classes with Joanna?" With her phone pressed to her ear and Hendrix in her lap, Grace repeated her daughter's story. In questions. "Dawn, this sounds like a made-for-TV movie. Are you sure it's true?"

"It's true, Mom. I'm sure. The girl goes...I mean...she *went* to the same school as Lisa's daughter. Everyone at Tinsley knows the story. It rocked the school. In fact, Lisa said people there are still talking about it."

"But then why is this girl at Oakdale High School?"

"Evidently the family has always lived here, but the kids went to private school in the city. Elizabeth, or 'Quinn', as she calls herself, was *encouraged* to leave Tinsley. Her parents must have scrambled and somehow gotten her into Oakdale."

"How come we didn't hear anything about it then? Wasn't it in the paper? Or online?"

"I asked Lisa the same questions," Dawn said. "It seems that the school tried to keep everything as hush-hush as they could. The teacher left quietly. And since the girl was a minor, and she wasn't formally charged due to lack of evidence, her name wasn't released to the public."

"But the people at Tinsley knew? The other students? The parents?"

"According to Lisa, yes. Unofficially, everyone knew."

"What about the damage to the teacher's car? It must have been totaled, right?"

"I assume so, and my guess would be that Quinn's parents probably handled everything as discretely as possible."

"That makes sense," Grace said. "And what about the parents? Do they still live in town? Are they together?"

"From what Lisa says, the gossip is that the father is a lot older than the mother, and he's very wealthy. Supposedly they have an open marriage, but Quinn didn't know that," Dawn said, "although maybe she does now."

"Hmm...well then, I think the most important question is whether this 'Quinn' is a girl who Joanna wants as a friend," Grace said, stroking Hendrix under his chin. He tilted his head back and purred. "If not, there's no problem, right?'

"Yeah, I guess," Dawn said slowly. "And I did get the feeling Joanna didn't like her very much. She rolled her eyes when she said her name, 'Quinn'. But then again, it's only been a couple of days. Things could change."

"True," Grace said. "Things can always change. But Joanna is a good girl with nice friends. Why would she, or any of her friends for that matter, want to get involved with someone like Quinn?"

Dawn sighed. "They wouldn't." She paused. "I guess."

"But then again..." Grace looked down at her now-sleeping cat and ran a hand down his back. "If *you* wouldn't know about Quinn's...uh...*history* if she hadn't gone to school with Lisa's daughter—"

"Oh jeez, you're right, Mom." Dawn cut her off. "Joanna and the other kids at Oakdale probably don't know either," she said, completing her mother's thought. "Do you think I should tell her?"

You're right, Mom.

Grace liked it when her daughter said those words, and she *loved* it when Dawn asked her for advice. But in this particular instance, she would rather not have been right, and she didn't have a clue about what advice to actually give.

Pushing a long stream of air out of her mouth, Grace went with her gut. "That's a tough call, Dawn. I trust Joanna, and I do believe she can keep a secret. But this one would be difficult," she said. "Plus, we don't know anything about the girl. Maybe she's on a better path, and she's trying to turn her life around."

"So, you don't think I should tell her?"

Grace closed her eyes and shook her head, glad this was a phone conversation and her daughter couldn't see her. Her first concern was for Joanna. But she also knew what it was like for a single mistake to...

She swallowed and then spoke, careful to phrase her answer as a question. "Maybe for now you shouldn't mention it?"

"Yeah, I guess that makes sense. Maybe I won't tell her. At least not right now," Dawn said. "Besides, I can always tell her later."

"Yes, you can. Just keep your eyes and ears open."

Dawn's response was quick. "And how do you suggest I do that? What do you mean?"

And just like that, Dawn reminded Grace of her own past behavior as a mother—the snooping, the eavesdropping, and the lack of respect for her daughter's privacy.

"Nothing, Dawn. I don't mean anything."

14

Quinn had become a permanent resident at Joanna's lunch table. Why though? It didn't make sense. Joanna couldn't understand why someone like Quinn would continue to sit at *her* table day after day. Sometimes it was an ordeal even for Joanna. Her girls were a group of misfits. That might sound harsh, but it was true.

Paige, who still had braces and probably would for another year, was a frantic hand-waver who thought she was smarter than she actually was. Megan needed to lay off the French fries, chocolate bars, and Lord knows what else, and Erin was a pretty enough girl whose parents' single goal was to keep their daughter safe from the big, bad world. Joanna had handpicked them to be her "friends," although in reality, they were more like an army of minions who did her bidding. They were a strange sort of "family," and the arrangement worked for them. But more importantly, it worked for Joanna.

"So, what do you guys do for fun around here?" Quinn

asked. Her eyes, rimmed with black liner, moved from Megan to Erin to Paige. She didn't look at Joanna.

Megan bit into her hamburger, and Paige coughed and reached for her water.

After a beat too long, Erin was the one to answer. "Just regular stuff. The mall, movies, get-togethers."

"What kind of get-togethers?"

"Like at someone's house," Erin said.

"Really? Whose house?"

Erin snuck Joanna a sidelong glance. But Joanna kept her face expressionless, letting Erin come up with her own answer.

"Sometimes Joanna's," Erin said, wiping her already clean mouth with a napkin.

"So, *you're* the party maker?" Quinn turned toward Joanna.

"Sometimes." Joanna shrugged a shoulder and raised her eyebrows. "Not recently though."

"What about the sleepover at your house, Joanna?" Megan leaned toward Joanna, her hamburger poised midair. "That was really––"

Joanna locked eyes with Megan, silently warning her not to say more.

But before Megan even had the chance to continue, Paige jumped in. "We were invited to Ryan's party last week. He's the guy who came over to the table before," she said a little too loudly. "The hot one."

"And?" Quinn asked.

Joanna crossed her arms in her lap and sat back in her chair, letting the scene play out.

"And...uh...something came up," Paige said, her face reddening. "I...uh...we didn't go."

Quinn's eyebrows shot up, and she tilted her head, fixing her gaze on Joanna. "And you didn't go either?"

"Nah," Joanna said, shaking her head.

"Okay." Quinn shrugged.

She was easy to read. Joanna knew the type. Quinn chose her questions carefully, rationing them out, and dug for information while feigning only a mild interest in the answer.

And Joanna knew what her next move would be.

Sure enough, Quinn looked down at her tray and stirred her yogurt. Waiting. Waiting for someone to ask the mysterious Quinn a question. And she didn't want to have her mouth full when that happened.

Paige was the one who gave Quinn what she wanted. It figured. Joanna could have predicted that too. Paige was always looking for more, for something better. You'd think she would have learned her lesson by now. Paige, the girl who couldn't even handle a little bit of extra pot in her brownie. Did she really think she'd be able to keep up with Quinn?

With her elbows on the table and her chin resting on her hands, Paige asked the question the white-haired newcomer had been waiting for. "So Quinn, what do you do for fun?"

Quinn popped a yogurt-filled spoon into her mouth and swallowed. "Mmm," she said, drawing out the moment. She licked her lips, placed her spoon on her napkin, and smiled. "Lots of things."

She was good. Joanna had to give her that.

"Like?" Paige asked.

"Well, it's different when you go to school in the city, you know?" Quinn rolled her shoulders back, glanced up at the ceiling, and opened her mouth in an exaggerated yawn. Then she turned her attention back to Paige. "There are parties somewhere every night, and there's always someone who can get you into a club. I still like to go, and I have plenty of friends who let me crash at their places."

Megan and Erin stared at Quinn, their heads tilted and their mouths partly open. They looked like a pair of little kids watching their first movie.

"Sounds awesome." Paige nodded, her eyes wide.

"Yeah, it does," Joanna chimed in, knowing that wasn't the response Quinn had expected.

Not from *her*.

Quinn cocked her head, her eyes narrowing, and licked her lips.

"So, why'd you want to transfer *here*?" Joanna asked. Her voice was sweet and smooth, masking the venom that both girls knew lurked beneath the innocent question. "I mean... to Oakdale?"

"Well," Quinn said, shifting in her seat, "After so many years of private school, I guess I just wanted a change, you know? And I still go into the city all the time. I might go back next year though. I don't know yet." She shrugged. "I'll figure it out."

Joanna didn't buy her answer. There was more to it than "wanting a change." But for the moment, she let it slide.

"Cool," she said with a quick nod.

"So, maybe the next time I go..." Quinn's voice trailed off. Drumming the table with her fingers, she glanced up at the ceiling. "We'll see," she said softly.

When the bell signaling the end of lunch period rang, Quinn was the first to jump up, and Paige rushed to follow close behind her as the group headed to the cafeteria door.

With a clumsy lurch, Paige reached for Quinn's elbow and leaned toward her. "Should I call you or email you the geometry homework?" she asked.

"Email's good," Quinn said with a close-mouthed smile that disappeared as soon as Paige looked away.

Joanna rolled her eyes and marched into the student-packed corridor.

∾

Fifteen minutes later, while Señora Lopez droned on in Spanish about the weather, Joanna didn't even try to concentrate.

Why was Paige doing Quinn's homework?

Quinn had aced the geometry test on her first day in class. And then there was her performance in the history bee. Obviously, she was very bright, and her private school's curriculum was more advanced than Oakdale's. She certainly didn't need Paige to do her homework. Joanna tapped her pencil against the cover of her notebook and stared at Señora Lopez's moving mouth.

Unless...unless it wasn't about the homework. Unless this was just Quinn's first step toward creating her own little family of followers. She'd dangled the possibility of an invitation to a New York City party with one hand while requesting homework answers with the other––the illusion of a reciprocal arrangement. She was good at the game, and that made her dangerous.

She was even able to identify Paige as the one most receptive to her strategy. The only problem was that Erin, Megan, and Paige belonged to Joanna. *She* was the one who had groomed them into loyal members of *her* little family. And no one, not even Quinn Chandler, with her bleached blonde hair, her ridiculous beret, and her overdone eyeliner, was going to change that.

No one.

15

G race and Joanna were up to 1968, the year of Dawn's birth, in the scrapbook. They sorted through pictures of Grace posing with her hands clamped on her hips, proudly displaying her swollen belly beneath paisley-printed dresses and tie-dyed shirts. Her hair, decorated with a daisy tucked behind an ear or topped with a red bandana, flowed long and loose. She had been a happy mother-to-be. An Earth goddess, as she'd been called back then.

Grace pulled out Dawn's faded birth certificate and her beaded newborn bracelet, the kind hospitals have since replaced with plastic wristbands. Grandmother and granddaughter pored over the rest of the pictures––Grace and Doug holding baby Dawn, feeding her, and gazing into her green eyes, tiny jade replicas of Grace's own.

Together, Grace and Joanna laid out the pages. Then, working side by side in an easy rhythm, they moved to the cutting, taping, and gluing phases. But something was bothering Joanna. Grace could see it. She could feel it. Joanna's mouth smiled, but her eyes were opaque, their familiar sparkle dulled. After they'd finished three pages, Grace scooped up a handful of markers and dropped them into the supply box.

Joanna leaned across the table and touched her grandmother's hand, crinkling her brow. "You don't want to do more, Grace-ma?" she asked.

"I don't know." Grace put her other hand on top of Joanna's and squeezed. "I thought we might stop for the day and just spend some time together. Maybe catch up a little?" she said. "I don't have such an interesting life, you know." She lifted her shoulders in a quick shrug. "I want to hear about yours."

"What makes you think my life is so interesting?" Joanna giggled.

"You're my granddaughter, Joanna. I love you, and I find everything about you interesting."

"Aw...Grace-ma..." Joanna jumped out of her chair and scurried around the table to her grandmother's side.

Grace swiveled in her seat, and their arms reached for each other, pulling their bodies together in a fierce hug that was strong, tight, and warm. Hendrix rubbed his soft fur against Grace's legs and meowed.

"Someone's jealous," Joanna whispered and bent to pick up Hendrix. She pressed him to her chest and stroked his back. "There, boy. We didn't forget about you," she said, and his meow turned into a purr.

"So then, what do you think about cookies and milk? I've got snickerdoodles," Grace offered, lifting an eyebrow. "For us, not him, that is," she added, petting the top of Hendrix's head.

"You know I'll never say no to that, Grace-ma. Not to

your cookies," Joanna said. "Snickerdoodles or any of them." She licked her lips, making a happy smacking noise.

After they packed up their scrapbooking supplies and wiped off the table, Grace and Joanna climbed onto the high rush-backed kitchen stools and settled into their usual spots in front of the center island. In tandem, they dipped their cookies into twin glasses of cold milk and bit into them, filling their mouths with the chewy, cinnamon sugar taste of homemade snickerdoodles.

"So, what's new?" Grace planted her elbows onto the table and swiveled her body toward Joanna. "Tell me what's been going on."

Joanna shrugged. "Not much. Just the regular stuff."

"School? Friends?' Grace prompted her. "Boys?"

After telling her grandmother that her homework was manageable, she was maintaining her "A" average, and Ryan was still annoying, Joanna mumbled something about a new girl, took a deep swallow of milk, and bit into a cookie, her long-lashed eyes staring down at the crumbs on her plate.

"Yes, Mom did tell me there was a new girl at school."

Joanna nodded, pushing a finger into a cookie crumb and popping it into her mouth.

"She said you didn't seem too happy about it though."

"I'm not." Joanna pressed her lips together and shook her head.

"Do you want to tell me why?" Grace asked gently.

Joanna sighed. "The new girl's name is Quinn, and I don't like her, Grace-ma." She paused. "I *really* don't like her," she said, a hard edge to her voice.

"Okay…" Grace said, waiting for more.

Joanna turned in her chair to face her grandmother directly. "She came from a private school in New York, and she has bleached blonde hair that looks white, and she wears this black beret all the time."

"So, she's not like your friends or the other kids in your school?"

"No, definitely not." Joanna spat out her answer through clenched teeth.

"Why don't you like her?"

"She's just so...I don't know...full of herself. She's really smart, and she's cool-looking in that city kind of way. That's not the problem though. It's her attitude." Joanna clicked her tongue. "It's hard to explain exactly."

"I'm listening," Grace said, putting her hand on her granddaughter's knee.

"She's sitting at my lunch table now. Paige invited her." Joanna rolled her eyes. "And now all the girls, *my* girls, especially Paige, but Erin and Megan too, hang on her every word. It's disgusting," she hissed.

"Hmm...I'm not sure I know what you mean by 'disgusting', Joanna," Grace said carefully. "Can you give me an example?"

Joanna's nostrils flared as the words tumbled out of her mouth. "Well, at lunch Quinn asked what we all do for fun, and of course, Paige asked her the same question. So, Quinn went on and on about going to parties and getting into clubs in New York. And then she hinted around about inviting us. Or maybe she just meant Paige, not the rest of us. I don't know." Joanna threw her hands up, letting them fall with a slap onto her blue-jeaned thighs. "Can you believe it? Why would she even do that?"

"I don't know why," Grace said, shaking her head slowly. "Could it be that she's just a new girl looking for friends?"

"It's more than that, Grace-ma. I know it. Why would a

girl like Quinn be interested in our little group? *My* group?" Joanna's knee bounced as she tapped her toe against the bottom rung of her stool. "She should want to hang out with the more popular girls." Her voice dropped. "You know Paige. And Erin and Megan. Why them?"

"Maybe it's not them, Joanna. Maybe it's *you* she's interested in."

"No, it's not me, Grace-ma." Joanna's head swung back and forth. "Quinn has a plan, and she's starting with Paige. She even has Paige doing her geometry homework. I heard them talking about it. But Quinn is really smart. She could do her own homework, no problem. I think it's something bigger," she said, tapping her cheek with a finger. "It's like she wants to take over, be in charge of the whole group. *My* group," she said, pointing to her chest. "And that is *not* going to happen." She brought her fisted hand down on the table.

Grace looked down at her granddaughter's clenched fist, and a chill prickled the back of her neck.

Joanna met Grace's eyes and opened her hand. Her face softened. "I'm sorry, Grace-ma. I-I'm overreacting. It really isn't that big a deal. I know my friends are my friends, and that's not going to change."

"No, Joanna, that's not going to change," Grace said calmly. "And as for the homework situation, cheaters ultimately get caught."

Joanna reached for a cookie and dunked it into her milk. "Yeah," she said quietly. "I suppose they do."

Several hours later, in the silent darkness of her bedroom, Grace rolled onto her side and stretched out her arm, groping along the night table for her white noise machine. She had bought it years ago to drown out the sound of Doug's snoring, but she still used it on restless nights. Switching it on, she tucked an extra pillow between her knees and curled into fetal position, waiting for sleep.

But sleep didn't come.

Grace should have been relieved. Joanna had absolutely no interest in developing any sort of relationship with Quinn, the bleached-hair private school refugee who might or might not be pursuing a friendship with Paige and the other girls. But something still gnawed at Grace, something even more disturbing than Dawn's original concern about the arrival of a possible teenage arsonist at Joanna's school.

Her conversation with her granddaughter replayed in her head like a stuck record—*my* girls, *my* group, *my* friends.

Somehow, Grace sensed that rather than the threat of losing their friendship, it was the thought of potentially losing her role as their leader that troubled Joanna. Her friends looked up to her, and they followed her. It had been that way since she'd been a child on the playground, leading the others from the sandbox to the slide and then on to the swing set.

Even though Grace was her grandmother, she was objective enough to see that Joanna had always been like the sun, pulling others into her orbit simply by *being*. She'd never been interested in joining the more popular cliques, although they would have welcomed her. No, Joanna had always preferred to select her own merry little band of followers.

Just like...

Grace felt a sudden shiver, and pulled her arms into her chest.

No, she wasn't just like...

Joanna was not like anyone. She was like herself. Grace's sweet, loving granddaughter.

Flicking on the light next to her bed, Grace sat up. She slid her feet into her slippers, stood up, and made her way to the bathroom medicine cabinet. She needed a sleeping pill.

heaters ultimately get caught. That's what Grace-ma said. Maybe she was right. But then again, maybe she was wrong. In Quinn's case, Joanna needed to make sure that her grandmother had been one hundred percent right.

Joanna didn't expect the geometry chapter test to be difficult. Mr. Reed had told the class the exam wouldn't involve proofs. So, it was merely a matter of understanding the questions and knowing how to apply the formulas which, of course, had to be memorized. For lots of people, that still wouldn't have been an easy task. Joanna knew some of her classmates cheated, although she'd never given much thought to how they did it.

Not BQ anyway.

Before Quinn.

It was actually pretty amazing––the stuff you could find out by googling. Students cheated by looking at each other's papers, sharing answers with hand signals, stealing teachers' master copies, and writing notes on their bodies, on cheat sheets, and even on the backs of erasers. Some of them used invisible ink. And those were just the more common techniques. The high-tech strategies were even more devious.

Joanna had done her research, and on the day of the test, she was ready. Sliding into her usual seat in the last row of Mr. Reed's classroom, she dropped her backpack onto the floor. She reached down and slipped her hand inside, feeling for her water bottle and running a finger along its label. It was glued on tight, no peeling edges. And it was the same brand Quinn always bought from the machine outside the cafeteria.

But this bottle was different. On the inside of its label, the formulas needed for the day's test had been neatly typed.

Wouldn't Mr. Reed be surprised when he discovered that his newest student, the one who had been challenging Joanna for top grade point average in his class, was a cheater!

Joanna had never seen him angry––face red and hands clenched. Or maybe he'd go the disappointed route––sad smile and slumped shoulders. Either way would be just fine. Oakdale High had a zero tolerance policy on cheating. A failing grade for the marking period and two days of suspension were mandatory punishments. Hopefully, that would be enough to send Quinn back to the fancy private school in New York where she belonged.

Joanna's skin tingled, and she tapped her pencil on her desk. Her plan was simple. After the tests were collected and the class dismissed, she'd tell Paige she needed to ask Mr. Reed something and have her go on ahead. She'd fumble in her backpack, making sure she was the last to leave. Definitely after Quinn. On her way out, she'd drop the water bottle on Quinn's desk. Mr. Reed had a free period after their class and usually stayed in the room to prep or grade papers. He'd have plenty of time to notice the lone water bottle left behind on his newest student's desk.

Paige settled into the seat beside Joanna. "So, you ready?"

Joanna nodded and popped a piece of gum into her mouth.

"You know the formulas?"

"Uh-huh."

"All of them?"

"Yup," Joanna said, the clean taste of spearmint filling her mouth.

Paige bent down to scratch her ankle, then looked up at Joanna, her eyebrows squished together. "Why do you have your backpack with you?"

"A couple of my teachers are making us bring our text-books to class today. So, it was easier for me stuff it all into my backpack than carry everything separately," Joanna spouted off her prepared answer.

"That makes sense," Paige said, her eyes trained on the door.

Joanna followed her gaze and watched the other students shuffle into the room. Just as the warning bell rang, Quinn dashed in. Paige waved at her and smiled, and Quinn, with a brisk lift of her hand, hurried to her seat. Mr. Reed shook his head, his lips pushed together, holding back a smile. He liked the smart ones. Like Joanna. And now Quinn.

But that was going to change. Very, very soon.

"Okay, everyone," Mr. Reed said, stepping in front of his desk and facing the class. "It's test time. Please put away your notes and textbooks."

The class emitted a collective groan, and Mr. Reed chuckled, playing out the familiar pre-test routine.

"Alright, people. No complaints." He started down the aisle closest to the window and made his way up and down the rows of desks, dropping a thin packet of stapled sheets face down in front of each student. "And please don't turn your tests over until I tell you to do so."

When the tests were distributed, he returned to the front of the room and leaned back against his desk, his eyes smiling along with his mouth. "You'll notice that I've given you a gift this time, guys. So, I expect high grades all around," he said. "You may turn your tests over and begin."

The room filled with the crinkly sound of rustling papers. Joanna flipped her test over and stared down at the first page.

It was a list.

A list of formulas.

From the perimeter of a polygon to the volume of a pyramid, from the easy ones Joanna had learned in middle school to the hard ones that even she had struggled to memorize, Mr. Reed had provided his students with a list.

A happy murmur rippled through the class, and pencils began to scratch their way across papers. Joanna's jaw went rigid, and her mouth tasted of metal. She breathed in and let the air out slowly, willing herself to relax, and looked down at her test. She gripped her pencil and forced herself to focus.

Mr. Reed collected the tests at the end of the period, and Joanna walked out of the classroom behind Paige. With a casual backward arm swing, she chucked her water bottle into the trash can next to the door.

She needed to come up with another plan, and she needed to do it soon.

"Where's Quinn?" Erin pointed to the empty seat at the lunch table and looked at Paige.

"She went home after the geometry test," Paige said. Then she leaned across the table and lowered her voice to a whisper. "Her mom signed her out for a doctor's appointment. But they're really going into the city to get her roots done. And to shop."

"She has to go into New York to get her roots done?" Joanna asked, rolling her eyes.

"Yes, Joanna. She has to go into New York to get her roots done," Paige said, her voice a sarcastic singsong. "She needs a special kind of processing, and she doesn't trust anyone out here to do it."

"Well, ex-cuuse me," Joanna said, tossing her head. "Guess I just don't know much about what it takes to turn your hair white."

"Whatever." Paige shrugged and dug a fork into her salad.

The table went silent, a quiet island in the noisy sea of cafeteria chatter that surrounded it. Erin, looking down at her lap, watched her fingers swat away imaginary crumbs, and Paige chomped on a mouthful of lettuce.

Megan took a deep swallow of iced tea and put down her glass, her eyes on Joanna. "So-o-o, what's up for the weekend?"

"I'm not sure yet. I'll think about it," Joanna said and turned toward Paige. "Do you have any ideas?"

Let's see what Ms. Wannabe Leader can come up with…

"Uh…not really, but…uh…I'm out for Saturday night," Paige said, her eyes darting from Joanna to Erin to Megan and then back to Joanna. She cleared her throat and swallowed. "Quinn invited me to sleep over."

Erin and Megan stared at her, their mouths falling open. A tiny twitch began in Joanna's right eyelid, and her chest tightened. She kept her gaze fixed on Paige and lifted her shoulders in what she hoped looked like an I-couldn't-careless kind of a shrug.

"Okay, that's fine. I'll do something with Erin and Megan," Joanna said evenly.

"But I can get together with you guys Friday night," Paige said.

Friday night? So now Paige was calling the shots? Was she delusional? Did she honestly think plans were going to be scheduled around her arrangements with Quinn? No, that was *not* going to happen. Joanna shook her head.

"Sorry, I'm busy Friday night," she said.

"What are you doing?" Paige asked.

What are you doing? It was a normal question, but under the circumstances...

"I'm seeing Grace-ma," Joanna said. A perfectly acceptable answer.

Friday night with Grace-ma. The idea had just popped into her head, but it was a good one. Her girls could come up with their own plans. Or not.

And as for Saturday night...she had an even better idea.

Moving quickly, Joanna plowed through the horde of students changing classes between fifth and sixth periods. Sure enough, Ryan stood at his locker. She'd passed him by dozens of times, never stopping. His hand reached for a book from the top shelf.

"Hey you," she said, touching his shoulder.

Ryan spun on his heel and turned to face her. His head jerked back, and his eyes widened. His lips curved into a slowly spreading smile.

"Hey *you*," he said, tapping Joanna's head with his book. "Make my day, and tell me you're looking for me." He wiggled his eyebrows.

Ryan was cute. Annoying sometimes, but still cute.

"Sorry, but I was just on my way to bio, and I saw you." Joanna pointed to her classroom down the hall.

"And you stopped," he said, stepping closer to her.

"Yes, that's true." She laughed. "I stopped."

"So?"

"So?" she said, repeating his question.

"So, when are you going to stop saying 'no' to me, Joanna?"

"That depends on what you're asking." She tilted her head, clamping her lips together and opening her eyes wide.

"I'm having people over Saturday night. Will you come?"

"Do you have people over *every* Saturday night?"

"Not 'every', but lots of times." He touched her elbow with his book. "So, will you come?"

"Can I bring a couple of friends?"

"If I say 'yes', will you come?"

"Uh-huh." Joanna nodded.

"Then it's a deal," he said, grabbing her hand and shaking it. "Now, get to class." With a happy grin, he reached behind her shoulder and tugged on her hair.

Yes, it was a deal.

17

"Come in, come in." Grace hugged her granddaughter as she stepped into the house. "It's such a treat for me to have you on a Friday night, Joanna. And for a sleepover, no less."

"It's a treat for me too, Grace-ma." Joanna squeezed Grace tight. "Oh, and Mom and Dad said they're sorry they couldn't come in. They're off to dinner with some friends."

"No problem. I'll see them tomorrow when they pick you up."

Joanna dropped her duffel bag by the door and followed her grandmother into the kitchen. They climbed onto the woven rush counter stools and began their milk and cookie ritual. Peanut butter oatmeal made from scratch. Still warm.

"So, what are your friends doing tonight?" Grace asked. "No plans for you girls?"

"Nothing special, and we're going to a party tomorrow. So, everyone's just hanging home tonight."

"And whose party is it, may I ask?"

"Ryan's." Joanna shrugged and bit into a milk-drenched cookie.

"Hmmm…"

Joanna giggled. "And what does 'hmmm' mean?"

It was Grace's turn to shrug, and she added an eye roll for good measure.

"I don't like him like *that*, Grace-ma. But he keeps asking me to his parties, so I decided to go this time."

"Are your three musketeers going too?"

Joanna exhaled, pushing her lips out, and shook her head. "Just Erin and Megan. Paige is sleeping at Quinn's house."

"*Quinn's* house?" Grace slapped her hand down on the counter. "Isn't she the new girl? The one you told me about?"

Joanna's eyes darkened into an opaque almost-black. She nodded, her lips pushed together, barely opening them to spit out a "Yup."

"I thought you girls didn't like her."

"*I* don't like her. But evidently some, or at least *one*, of us does," Joanna said. "Figures it would be Paige," she added in a gruff mutter.

"Joanna, sweetie, listen to me." Grace reached for her granddaughter's hand. "You have long-standing friendships. Erin and Megan love you, and they're loyal to you. So is Paige." She glanced down at their intertwined fingers, hers pale and freckled, Joanna's olive-toned and smooth—the generations in their hands. "You don't like Quinn, and you don't have to. But Paige might feel differently, and you need to be okay with that." She looked up at Joanna and smiled. "Plus, a party at Ryan's sounds a lot more interesting than a sleepover at Quinn's."

"I guess." Joanna said, her mouth shaped into a half-smile, her eyes unreadable. "Anyway, let's work on the scrapbook."

"Good idea!"

Tonight––the scrapbook. And tomorrow, Grace would talk to Dawn. Maybe it was time for Joanna to learn just a little bit more about the new girl in school.

∾

"Let's see. Where are we up to?" Grace flipped through the scrapbooked pages of her life.

"Grace-ma!" Joanna jumped up, planting her hands on her hips. "We're at the summer of 1969! Remember what that is?" She grinned.

"I remember." Grace closed her eyes and nodded.

Joanna dug through the large box of photos and memorabilia that had already been sorted by event and year and pulled out a thick manila envelope marked *Woodstock, 1969*. She unwound the twine wrapped around the envelope and gently turned it over, letting its contents spill out across the table.

A mud-splattered concert program, a pair of ticket stubs, a copy of *LIFE* magazine's special Woodstock Music festival edition––its cover decorated with the famous bird on a guitar logo––and a stack of photos taken with her grandmother's Instamatic camera. Joanna studied the program, ran her fingers over the ticket stubs, and slowly turned the pages of the commemorative magazine.

"Woodstock," she whispered. "Grace-ma, you were there."

"Yes," Grace said, tilting her head and smiling. "I was there."

Joanna scooped up the pile of photos, sifting through the faded and blurry images of a faraway stage, a sea of people, and Grace and Doug, both looking impossibly young.

"Look at this!" Joanna giggled and slid one of the pictures over to Grace. "How did you ever get Grandpa Doug to wear a bandana?"

Grace looked down at the photo. She and Doug, looking like kids although by then they were already teenage parents, dressed in the matching tie-dyed t-shirts Grace had created in the bathtub. Doug's too-short-for-Woodstock hair was covered with a bandana, and Grace's blonde braids were strung through with daisies. Their faces were suntanned and freckled, their mouths stretched into euphoric smiles.

Grace thumbed through the other pictures. Even in the rain-soaked ponchos Doug had insisted on packing "just in case," the young couple beamed with the joy of being together in a magical place at a magical time.

"I think the bigger question is how did I ever get him to *go*?"

"That's true." Joanna bobbed her head up and down in a brisk nod. "How did you?"

"It wasn't easy." Grace shook her head, smiling at the memory. "But he knew how much *I* wanted to go. And part of the reason for that was because I wanted him to see Janis Joplin and Jefferson Airplane like I had with Paula in San Francisco. Then, when my parents offered to take care of your mother for the weekend, he didn't have an excuse not to go."

"So, what did he think?"

"Well, he called it 'an experience'. But actually, I think his favorite part of the whole thing was *telling* people that he was there." Grace laughed.

"And Mom's favorite part is telling people that you left her home."

Joanna and Grace looked at each other and burst into laughter.

"That's absolutely true. We did not take your infant mother to Woodstock," Grace said, catching her breath. "But c'mon now, we've got work to do."

Sitting side by side, they arranged the pictures on the scrapbook pages, decorating their borders with stick-on flowers and peace signs. They slipped the concert program, the ticket stubs, and the copy of *LIFE* magazine into plastic sleeves.

"This scrapbook is really coming out great, Joanna," Grace said. "It was such a wonderful gift, and I love that we're doing it together."

"Me too, Grace-ma." Joanna scrunched her shoulders and leaned forward, her hands clasped in her lap. "And I thought of something we could add to it," she said, drumming her feet against the floor. "I brought it with me."

"Hmm...Now, I'm curious." Grace tapped her mouth with a finger and leaned back in her chair.

Joanna jumped out of her seat and hurried to the door. Grace waited in the kitchen, and Joanna came back with her duffel bag draped over her arm. Hendrix trotted along behind her and rubbed up against Grace's leg.

"So?" Grace said, reaching down to run her hand down Hendrix's back.

Joanna pulled a blue folder out of the bag and set it on the table. "I went online and searched out some of the important events that happened during your lifetime. I thought we could put in some pages with newspaper headlines and pictures to kind of anchor everything in time.

Historic time." She lifted her eyebrows, her eyes wide. "What do you think?"

"'What do I think?'" Grace repeated her question. "I think that's a fantastic idea!" She reached for Joanna and pulled her into a tight hug. "What a brilliant and creative granddaughter I have!"

Joanna kissed Grace's cheek, squeezed her shoulder, and stepped back. "Oh, good. I'm so happy you like it. These are just a few of the things I came up with so far." She handed the folder to Grace. "And I know you don't like the Beatles, Grace-ma, so I left out the article I found about their arrival in the U.S." She wagged her finger in the air. "Even though it was history."

Grace smirked and opened the folder, her eyes widening as she began to flip through the stack of pages emblazoned with headlines, articles, and photos. "Wow! I can't believe you did all this, Joanna!"

> *Polio vaccine created, 1952*
> *School segregation ruled illegal in the U.S., 1954*
> *Elvis Presley's first appearance on The Ed*
>   *Sullivan Show, 1956*
> *John F. Kennedy assassinated, 1963*
> *Martin Luther King and Robert F. Kennedy*
>   *assassinated, 1968*
> *The Manson Family murders, 1969*

The Manson Family murders...

Charlie Manson stared out from the page, his opaque black eyes, flared nostrils, and a devilishly raised right eyebrow a macabre counterpoint to the oddly relaxed line of his mouth.

Grace's throat went dry, and her hand froze mid-air. Across time and space, he could haunt her still. She coughed, choking and gulping air, and her eyes began to water and sting.

Joanna patted her back. "Grace-ma, are you okay?"

Grace cleared her throat and pressed her hand to her chest. "I'm fine." She swallowed. "Just something tickling my throat."

"Do you want a cough drop?" Joanna sprung out of her chair. "They're in the pantry, right?" she asked, already halfway across the kitchen.

"No, no. I'm fine, Joanna," Grace said. "Really."

"What about a glass of water?"

"Maybe." Grace's voice came out in a hoarse croak. "Okay."

Joanna filled a glass from the filtered pitcher in the refrigerator and set it in front of her grandmother. "Here, Grace-ma," she said, touching Grace's shoulder.

Grace wrapped her fingers around the glass, tilted her head back, and drank, letting the cold water wash down her scratchy throat. Joanna watched, her eyebrows lowered and her eyes clouded with concern. Grace finished drinking and ran her tongue across her lips.

"Are you okay?" Joanna asked.

An icy shiver rippled down Grace's back, and her scalp prickled with a sudden chill. Wrapping her arms across her chest, she swallowed and inhaled deeply. "I'm fine. Nothing to worry about. But I do feel like I might be coming down with something," she said. "Would you mind if we finish this up next time?"

"No, of course not." Joanna said and began to scoop the pages splashed with photos and headlines back into the folder. "We can work on it at my house when my parents go away."

Grace reached across the table and squeezed her granddaughter's warm hand. "Yes, we'll do it then." she whispered, her voice raspy and thin.

PART II

18

W ith her wallet in hand, Grace stepped onto the bus. "Could I get a round trip to New York?" she asked the driver. "Senior citizen, please."

"You were supposed to buy the ticket at the kiosk over there." He pointed to the awning-covered shelter where Grace had been waiting.

"I'm sorry. I didn't realize that."

"Never mind." He shook his head. "The fare is twelve dollars."

Grace pulled a ten and two singles out of her wallet and handed them to him. "Thank you."

He grunted and handed her a ticket for the return trip.

She thanked him again and turned to make her way down the aisle. With a jerk, the bus veered away from the curb, sending her off balance. Her body lurched forward in a teetering two-step. She reached for the top edge of the closest seat and plopped down into it.

Not an auspicious beginning for her trip into the city.

Or for her meeting with Paula.

The bus merged onto the highway. Grace closed her eyes

and leaned back against the seat. Relax, she commanded herself, and she slipped into a fitful half-snooze.

The bus slowed, its speed reduced to a crawl, and Grace snapped into wakefulness. Turning her head to the window, she gazed at the line of cars, trucks, and buses jockeying for position as they fought to enter one of the few narrow lanes leading into the Lincoln Tunnel. Its gray arched entrance loomed up ahead.

In less than half an hour, she would meet Paula.

It would be a journey into Grace's past, into their shared past. And while almost all of her memories of the "us" that was Paula-and-Grace were happy and good, there was one particular moment in time, a nightmare moment they both had shared, that Grace had kept hidden away for more than half a century. It was something that had happened, and it had happened a long, long time ago. A lifetime ago.

But it had indeed happened.

The bus moved into the tunnel, and the world turned into a straight-lined subterranean path bordered by tiled walls and rows of overly bright lights.

More than fifty years had gone by, and Grace still remembered the weather that day, the temperature in the low 70's and the bright blue sky dotted with high, puffy clouds. Typical early summer weather for San Francisco and perfect for a visit to Golden Gate Park.

Decked out in the Indian print dresses, long beaded necklaces, and huarache sandals they'd bought on Ashbury Street, Grace and Paula had dressed for the occasion. Feathery earrings dangled from Grace's ears, and a thin headband bisected Paula's forehead. Slouchy macramé bags hung from their shoulders.

"C'mon, it's this way." Paula tugged on Grace's hand, leading her deeper into the park.

Grace followed her friend up the sloping green lawn and onto the grassy rise the locals called "Hippie Hill." The wide-open area, bordered by large leafy trees, was overlaid with a patchwork quilt of long-haired young people clothed in blue jeans, floppy hats, military jackets, ponchos, fringed vests, and shirts embroidered with the colors of the rainbow. The air crackled and hummed like it was shot through with electricity. It was the most alive place Grace had ever seen. She stood still. Spellbound.

"Don't just stand there, Gracie." Paula laughed. "Let's go."

"Yeah!" Grace nodded. "Let's go." She raced ahead, jumped into the air, and spun around.

Paula caught up to Grace and grabbed her arm, and laughing together, they set out to explore "the Hill." They strolled past a bearded man singing "Puff, the Magic Dragon" and a circle of women sitting cross-legged on the grass, their faces tilted up to the sun. A tall man, made even taller by his outsized Afro, lifted his hand in a peace sign wave as they passed, and a ponytailed couple, his hair longer than hers, brandished hand-lettered signs.

Make Love, Not War

Power to the People

"Paula, this place is like...I don't know. I feel like I'm in some sort of..." Grace paused, searching for the right words. "Surrealistic wonderland?"

Paula's mouth stretched into a wide grin. "Yup, that's one way of—"

"Paula!" A voice called out from behind them.

Moving in tandem, Grace and Paula whirled around and spotted the smiling girl skipping toward them. Her waist-length hair was a golden shade of red that gleamed in the sun.

"Wendy!" Paula squealed.

"I thought that was you."

Paula grinned and nodded. "It's me alright, and this is Grace." She hooked her arm through her friend's.

"Like Grace Slick from Jefferson Airplane?" Wendy laughed.

"I wish." Grace smirked.

"Well, I'm Wendy. Like Wendy from *Peter Pan*." She spread her arms wide and pirouetted in a patchouli-scented twirl.

"Wendy works in a head shop at the corner of Haight and Ashbury. It's the coolest place in the world," Paula said, bouncing up on her toes.

Wendy threw her arms up and giggled. "Feed your head, you know?"

"Mm-hmm," Paula agreed, her eyes sparkling, and pulled Grace closer. "Grace is my friend from New Jersey."

"Hey there, Grace from New Jersey. I'm from Pennsylvania." Wendy smiled. "Lots of people are coming in from the East these days. By car, van, bus, or even by thumb. Everyone's trying to find a way to move out here, you know. And *you* made it." She clapped her hands together. "You're gonna––"

"Oh no, I'm not moving here." Grace shook her head. "I'm just out for a few weeks visiting Paula."

"You're just visiting?" Wendy stared.

"Uh-huh." Grace nodded.

"Why?" she asked. "Why aren't you staying?"

"Um, well, I have a boyfriend at home, and I'm going to college, and…" Grace's voice trailed off.

"Okay, that's your decision, babe. It's crazy, but it's up to you." Wendy shrugged. "But hey, as long as you're here, there's someone I want you to meet. Both of you actually," she said. "C'mon." She held out her hand, a stack of silver bracelets adorning her wrist.

Leading Paula and Grace past a mixed bag of people playing instruments, singing, reciting poetry, or simply walking through the park, wide-eyed and smiling, Wendy stopped in front of a small tree topped with a wide, almost horizontal, leafy canopy. Under its shade, a dark-haired man sat Buddha-style, strumming the battered guitar that rested across his knees and singing. His voice was clear and smooth.

"Charlie?" Wendy leaned down and whispered.

The man looked up, his eyes moving from Wendy to Paula to Grace. Wendy rose to her full height, and the three girls stood before him, frozen in their places. Then he smiled, his cheeks dimpling above his short beard.

"Charlie, this is Paula and Grace." Wendy said. "They wanted to meet you."

"Then I want to meet them," he said softly. "Welcome to my corner of the universe, girls." With one hand still on his guitar, he swept his other through the air. "What do you seek here?"

Grace shot Paula a sidelong glance, catching her looking down at her feet.

"What do we all seek, Charlie?" Wendy responded with her own question.

"Truth? Peace? Meaning? Wisdom?" His eyes closed and opened in a slow blink. "Love?"

"All of the above?" Grace said.

"Yes. All of the above." Charlie's eyes lasered into hers.

"We call Charlie 'The Gardener'. He takes care of all the flower children in the Haight," Wendy said, dipping her head in what looked more like a bow than a nod.

Grace didn't understand what Wendy meant, but she wanted to learn more, and she wanted to know Charlie. There was something special about him. More than special. He had the power of a mystical magnet, pulling her toward him. Grace looked over at Paula, her lips parted and her eyes bright, and she knew her friend felt it too.

Charlie smiled, close-mouthed like a male Mona Lisa. Like he knew something the rest of them didn't. And even back then, maybe he did.

～

Charlie invited Paula and Grace to his house that night. He dug into his pocket, handed them each a brown plastic guitar pick and said, "Cole Street, Number 636."

"Are your parents going to be okay with that?" Grace asked Paula as they left the park.

"Sure. I'll just tell them we're going to a party at Wendy's and crashing at her pad." She grinned. "She said we could do that if it got late."

"Do they know Wendy?"

Paula stopped and turned to face her friend. "Gracie, this isn't New Jersey. Even my parents have gotten hipper. It must be something in the San Francisco air." She laughed. "Trust me, it won't be a problem. And why would they worry anyway? What could happen?"

She was right, Grace thought. What could happen?

～

"You ready?" Paula touched Grace's elbow as they stood in front of 636 Cole Street. The address Charlie had given them was just a short walk from the corner of Haight and Ashbury.

Grace gazed up at the Victorian style row house. It looked like one of those places TV newscasters in jackets and ties pointed to when they broadcast stories about "hippies" who played their music too loud, had sex with each other, and protested the war. Oh, and they did drugs too.

Paula was right. This was not New Jersey. And yes, Grace was ready. She pulled her Instamatic out of her bag and snapped a photo of the house.

"Why are you taking a picture?" Paula asked.

Grace shrugged. "I don't know."

And she truly didn't know. Six thirty-six was one of a row of similar houses on Cole Street. But she was there, an invited guest, and she wanted a picture.

The girls climbed the shallow steps leading up to the door. Paula pressed her finger to the bell, but it refused to ring. Grace reached out and knocked softly. An intoxicating mixture of rock music, laughter, and indecipherable conversation wafted out of the old Victorian, but Grace's knock went unanswered.

Paula pounded on the door, her open hand smacking against the wood. Just as she stopped to rub her throbbing hand, a dull thump-thump heralded approaching footsteps. The door swung open, and a barefoot girl with a tangle of auburn hair looked at the visitors, her face a blank stare.

"Hi." Paula stepped toward her, tugging Grace along. "I'm Paula, and this is Grace."

The girl stood rooted to the floor, unmoving.

Paula dug into her bag and pulled out the guitar pick Charlie had given her earlier. "Charlie asked us to stop by."

The girl's eyes opened wide at the mention of Charlie's name. "Oh, come in then," she said, sweeping her hand back in a welcoming arc.

So many times over the years that had passed since that night, Grace had asked herself the same questions...Had she felt any doubt? A flash of uncertainty? A hint of dread? The cold finger of warning trailing down the back of her neck? The answer to all of those questions was always the same. No, no, no, and no. She had been an eighteen-year-old girl from New Jersey visiting her best friend in California. Neither one of them had had any qualms whatsoever about walking into that house.

Charles Manson's house.

Grace and Paula followed the girl into a crowded room packed with things and people. Long-haired guys and sleepy-eyed girls in thrift shop hippie garb sprawled on tattered couches, leaned against paint-peeling walls, or sat cross-legged like underfed Buddhas. A cable spool table strewn with rolling papers, candy wrappers, and a half-empty pack of cigarettes squatted in the center of the room, and a curtain of long wooden beads hung over the arched doorway that led deeper into the house. A scattered collection of flickering candles fitted into Mateus bottles added an eerie glow to the dimly lit space, and the Beatles sang about "getting by with a little help from their friends" from a small stereo system. The combined smells of pot, incense, tobacco, and unwashed bodies hung in the air.

Wendy, her head resting on the shoulder of a tall guy in a striped shirt, lifted her hand in a lazy wave, and Paula and Grace, their mouths curved into matching smiles, waved back. Wendy motioned them over, and they sank into the empty floor pillows beside her, catty-corner from a small bookshelf stocked with dusty paperbacks. *How to Win*

Friends and Influence People, *Stranger in a Strange Land*, and a bunch of others.

The beaded curtain strings parted with a crackly rustle, and everyone in the room turned toward the arched doorway. Their eyes fixed on Charlie as he strode into the room. Dressed in a denim shirt and jeans, his body short and wiry, his movements were deliberate. Controlled and controlling. They were all on his turf, and they knew it. Every single one of them.

Charlie's head moved in a slow swivel as he surveyed the scene, locking eyes with each person, one by one, then moving to the next. He crossed the room and gracing those in his path with nods and head pats, he headed directly to Paula and Grace. Reaching for Paula's left hand and Grace's right, he brought them into a circle of three.

"Welcome, children," he said softly, squeezing their hands. "Welcome to the family."

Charlie's eyes radiated warmth and power. Grace felt pulled into that place, that time, those people, that man. She felt like she was exactly where she needed to be.

They smoked pot and drank Kool-Aid. Charlie talked about freedom and love. His voice moved from a whisper to a roar, and his arms swept through the air in graceful arcs. Closing his eyes, he began to spin in a trancelike whirl as the Beatles sang "Lucy in the Sky with Diamonds."

Grace heard a rainbow of colors in the music, and a river of peace and calmness flowed through her body. She looked down into her lap and watched as the Indian print of her dress began to magically pulse and change colors. She was awake. Alive. Energized. She was ready.

And suddenly, she was dancing, the music miraculously inside of her, guiding her. Paula, Wendy, the barefoot girl with the auburn hair, the tall guy in the striped shirt, and all the others, long-haired and blue-jeaned.

And Charlie. Always Charlie. Together and apart. They danced.

A sharp tap on her shoulder followed by another startled Grace awake. She opened her eyes to Paula's upside-down face hanging over her own. Her friend's skin was pale, and beads of sweat dotted her forehead. Grace blinked and yawned, arching her back.

"Ow!" she yelped as her shoulders hit the hard floor.

"Gracie, we need to go."

"W-Why?" she asked, closing her eyes.

"Gracie, open your eyes," Paula said. "Now."

There was something in her voice.

Grace's eyes snapped open, and she forced herself up into a sitting position. Turning her head, which seemed filled with cotton, she scanned the jumble of sleeping bodies strewn across the room like discarded dolls. Some clothed, some not, they lay on their backs, on their sides, curled up into fetal balls, spread-eagled, or entwined as couples. Sunshine seeped through the room's dirty blinds, striping the bodies with slants of light.

"What time is it?" Grace asked.

Paula looked down at her watch. "It's nine. Let's go, Gracie."

"Where's Charlie?" she asked. "Where's Wendy?"

"I don't know. I haven't seen them."

Grace looked around the room again, more slowly this time. "What's going on, Paula?"

Paula shook her head, and her lower lip trembled. "I don't know, Gracie. Just get up. Let's go."

Grace got to her feet and faced Paula. The strap of her friend's dress had fallen off her shoulder, and Grace reached out to slide it back into place, but she couldn't. The strap had been ripped off, its unattached edge ending in a jagged tear. Paula's eyes glistened, and Grace looked away.

She smoothed her own dress down over her thighs, but something felt different. *She* felt different. There was an open airy space between her legs coupled with a raw soreness deep inside.

Something had happened. Something bad.

She pressed her hands to her hips, feeling her body beneath the thin fabric of her dress. A metallic taste invaded her mouth, and her heart began to pound against her chest, threatening to burst out of it in a fiery explosion.

Her underwear was gone.

Grace spent a few more weeks with Paula in San Francisco. They visited Alcatraz, Fisherman's Wharf, and a couple of museums that Grace no longer remembered the names of. All the touristy places. They rode cable cars, and Paula's father drove them down the zigzag turns of Lombard Street. They never went back to Golden Gate Park or to 636 Cole Street.

Grace returned to New Jersey, and by summer's end, she discovered she was pregnant. She married Doug, the father of her unborn child. She checked her calendar, and she was sure of that. Doug, her high school boyfriend. The father of her child. Grace was sure. Absolutely sure.

Dawn was born in the spring. Grace had wanted to

name her "Star," but Doug vetoed it. So, they settled on "Dawn" as a first name and "Star" as a middle. Dawn Star Raymond. And Doug was right about "Star." Dawn never did like her middle name.

Stepping into marriage and motherhood was an easy and natural move for Grace. She and Doug had been in love for what, at the age of eighteen, had seemed like forever, and with a baby on the way, that love deepened in ways that neither of them could have imagined as just half of a high school couple. She put her college dreams on hold, replacing them with other, and in her mind, bigger dreams.

Grace wasn't sure exactly when it was that she fell in love with her daughter. Did it happen as soon as she learned she was pregnant? Or was it the first time she felt a flutter deep inside her belly? Was it the moment that, with a scream and a massive push, she finally brought her newborn child into the world? Or was the lifelong love that Grace felt for Dawn only truly born the first time she held the tiny body in her arms? She didn't know, and it didn't matter.

Attentive without being smothering, Grace was the relaxed and calm mother of a happy, smiling child. She, Doug, and Dawn moved in an easy rhythm, and their world was safe and good.

When the Manson murders were committed in the summer of 1969, no one called them that. Not yet. The identities of the savage killers of Sharon Tate, Jay Sebring, Abigail Folger, Wojciech Frykowski, and Stephen Parent on August 9 and of Leno and Rosemary LaBianca the following evening would remain unknown until the late fall of that year. It was only then that Charles Manson and a hand-picked group of his followers would be identified as culprits in one of the most sensational murder cases of the century.

Charles Manson.

Charlie Manson.

The Charlie Manson who had lived at 636 Cole Street during the summer of 1967. The Charlie Manson who had invited Grace to visit. The Charlie Manson who...

And all of a sudden, something changed. Grace changed. She became watchful. Vigilant. She worried about her daughter, and as she grew, Grace snooped, she eavesdropped, and she disrespected Dawn's privacy. She was beyond cautious. She was obsessed. Guilty for something that had never happened.

It couldn't have.

Dawn had Grace's green eyes and Doug's light brown hair. She was so obviously their daughter, a sunny-tempered and beautiful combination of the best of both of them. You could tell just by looking at her. Everyone said so. Plus, Grace had done the math. She had checked the calendar. There was no way. No way at all. And yet, she had spent so many years worrying.

Worrying about something that was absolutely impossible.

∽

The bus pulled into the terminal, and Grace followed a stony-faced and silent middle-aged couple down the aisle toward the door.

She thanked the driver and stepped into the Port Authority. Immediately, she was accosted by lights, noise, and people. Lots of people. All rushing, all looking like they knew where they were going.

Grace hadn't been to New York since Tom and Dawn had taken her and Joanna to a Broadway show a couple of years earlier. Tom had driven, dropped them at the theater while he parked the car, and then whisked them off to an over-priced restaurant where they ate mediocre food. But, *this* was an altogether different place, and Grace was here for an altogether different reason.

She adjusted the strap on her shoulder bag, converting it into a crossbody, and pressed it tightly against her thigh. Scanning the crowd of people, all on their way to some-where else, Grace hurried over to a young woman waiting in line for the restroom. Brave girl, she thought. The woman was looking down at her phone, but so was everyone else on the line except for a gray-haired lady in a purple raincoat who appeared to be having a heated conversation—with herself.

"Excuse me, do you know where I can find the Grey-hound station?" Grace asked the woman with the phone.

"One level down. You'll see the signs," she said, glancing up at Grace.

"Thank you," Grace said, but the woman's eyes were already back on her phone, her thumbs tapping away.

Grace took the escalator down, followed the signs, and entered the Greyhound terminal. The place was jam-packed with people. They waited in departure lines, poured out of arriving buses, and sprawled on grated metal chairs. Most of them were either wheeling or guarding suitcases—striped, flowered, or solid-colored in black, red, blue, and even a neon orange.

Grace made a beeline for the single empty seat in a row of attached chairs facing Paula's arrival door, settling herself between a gum-chewing teenage boy and a thirty-some-thing woman wearing jeans and dirty white sneakers. Neither of them made eye contact with her as she lowered herself into the seat. She looked down at her watch. Paula's bus was due to arrive in seven minutes.

Grace hadn't seen Paula since Dawn was a baby. A few months after the summer Grace had visited her in San Francisco, Paula moved to a commune. Over the years, she'd traveled a bit and fallen in love with a string of wild and undependable men, ultimately replacing them with a succession of increasingly dangerous drugs. She did come back to New Jersey for Grace and Doug's wedding and one more time for a quick visit when Dawn was a baby. The former friends kept in touch sporadically for a few years after that. But eventually, they found themselves with less and less to say to each other, and they disappeared from each other's lives.

Slipping her hand into her bag, Grace reached for her book, wrapping her fingers around its smooth cover. But no, she couldn't concentrate on reading. She pulled her hand out, abandoning the book, and moved her bag into her lap, resting it across her jiggling thighs. Her mouth was dry. She swallowed, but it didn't help. Of course, she was nervous to meet the friend she hadn't seen in so many years. That was natural. More than half a lifetime had gone by since their last meeting. They had both grown up. They had aged. Would they even recognize each other if this were some kind of accidental, bumping-into-you kind of rendezvous?

But it wasn't the gray in her hair or the little lines on her face that were making Grace's thighs twitch and her mouth go dry. She wasn't concerned about today at all. It was that other day, that other night––what she and her friend had done and what had been done to them––that sent an icy shiver down her spine. She pulled her shawl closer to her body and wrapped her arms across her chest.

The minutes dragged by. The gum-chewer headed for one of the glass doors, and a bald man with a thick mustache claimed his empty seat. Grace checked her watch again. The bus was late. She crossed her legs and leaned back in her seat, her dangling foot bouncing up and down in a jerky rhythm.

Her new neighbor leaned toward her and touched her knee. "Excuse me, ma'am. Would you mind not jiggling your foot? It's making me nervous."

Grace yanked her knee back from his hand. "Sorry," she said, uncrossing her legs and angling her body away from him.

The arrivals door for Paula's bus finally burst open, and Grace sprang out of her seat. One by one, the bus-weary travelers, lugging suitcases, carryalls, and backpacks, stepped into the terminal, their eyes blinking in the artificial brightness. Grace scanned their faces—young, old, and in between cast in a rainbow of colors—searching for Paula's. The people poured in, and she didn't see her friend until...

An overweight woman with frizzy eggplant-colored hair broke free from the crowd, and smiling and waving, rushed toward her. "Gracie!" she shrieked, dropping her suitcase and pulling Grace into her arms.

Grace's body stiffened, pressed against this unfamiliar woman who must have been her old friend. "Paula," she said, forcing herself to return the woman's hug.

"Let me take a look at you, Gracie," Paula crowed, stepping back and clamping her hands onto Grace's shoulders. "Jeez, you look the same as I remember you. Is there some kind of fountain of youth in New Jersey?" She laughed, her voice erupting into the high-pitched giggle Grace remembered so well, erasing the years between them. Almost.

"And you," Grace said, reaching out to touch Paula's hair. "I love your hair," she said, offering the compliment she thought she should.

"Got tired of the mousy brown. Especially after the gray started coming in."

"Paula, there's never been anything mousy about you." Grace shook her head. "Not your hair. Not your personality. Not anything."

"Well," Paula said, her face turning serious. "That's not always a good thing."

"Why not?"

"Hmm...uh...let's just say I've had a...well..." She paused, looking up at the ceiling for a moment before turning her gaze back to Grace. "I've had a colorful life, Gracie," she said slowly.

Grace swallowed and nodded, not quite sure what to say to the woman, no longer a girl, who had once been her best friend. But that was a long time ago. And they both knew it.

"Anyway," Paula's voice turned bubbly. "I've got a couple of hours before I have to leave. Are you up for a nice long lunch?"

"That's just what I had in mind," Grace said, not sure if it was actually true. "Do you want to find a place to store your suitcase first?"

But that wasn't as easy as it sounded. When a policeman, with a series of complicated directions, told them that all luggage storage facilities were located *outside* of the terminal, they settled on a brightly lit restaurant inside the building.

They ordered sandwiches and iced teas, and a tired-looking waitress scooped up their menus and strolled toward the kitchen.

Sliding her chair closer to the table, Grace leaned toward Paula. "So? Tell me. What have you been doing for the past...uh...I-don't-know-how-many years?"

And so their long-delayed conversation began. Grace listened to Paula's saga of "getting back to the land" on a commune in northern California, traveling cross-country in a VW bus with an alcoholic boyfriend, moving to Atlanta with a man who swore he had been divorced...twice, and painstakingly crawling out of the nightmare world of drugs, booze, and abusive men that she had fallen into.

"I had no idea, Paula." Grace's chest tightened, and tears pricked at her eyes. "You've been through so much. I just knew a small piece of it. I..." She shook her head.

"I know you had no idea. We had already drifted apart and lost contact. Our lives went in different directions. It happens." Paula shrugged. "Anyway, today I'm clean, and my life is beginning to come together. But enough about all that." She flicked her hand out into the air, waving her past away. "You know, I still have all the letters you wrote me after I moved to California. Every. Single. One," she said, tapping the table three times to punctuate her words.

"And guess what?" Grace smiled, thinking of her own ribbon-tied bundle of letters tucked away in the bottom drawer of her night table. "I saved all of yours too."

"A letter a week, at least three sheets of notebook paper. That's what we did. Remember?"

"I do." Grace nodded. "And the things we wrote about... the Beatles vs. the Monkees, the newest TV shows, our teachers, boys—"

"Ah...boys...but for you, Gracie, it was always about Doug."

"Yes, it was," Grace said. "Except for that one time...I think it lasted about a week...the new boy in my English class...what was his name?" She propped her elbow on the table and lowered her chin to her hand.

"Hmm...?"

"Kevin!" they blurted out in unison.

"Great minds..." Grace said, tapping her temple.

"Yup." Paula agreed. "And now it's your turn," she said. "Tell me about you. And you better show me pictures." She wagged her finger.

Grace pulled out the stack of photos she had stashed in her bag in preparation for the day, and between bites of her sandwich and sips of tea, she updated her old friend on the doings of Dawn, Joanna, and Tom. She told Paula about Doug, their life together, and how much she still missed him. She handed her the pictures, a two-dimensional and incomplete documentary of the last fifty years of her life.

Paula smiled as she flipped through shots of Dawn with a missing front tooth, then in a ballet tutu, and later posing in the driver's seat of her first car. "She looks a lot like both you and Doug," she said. "She's a very pretty girl."

"Thanks, Paula. I think she got the best of both of us." Grace's mouth stretched into a wide grin.

The next picture was Dawn and Tom's wedding portrait. And then, there was a shot of baby Joanna smiling into the camera. Paula stared at the photo, looked up at Grace, and then back down at the picture.

"She's beautiful," she said quietly. "But she doesn't look like you at all. Dawn either." She tilted her head and turned back to the picture of Dawn and Tom. "Or her father. Her hair and her eyes...they're so dark."

Grace watched as Paula thumbed through the remaining pictures––Joanna as a toddler in a striped bathing suit, as a little girl with a red lollipop, and a recent shot of her cradling Hendrix in her lap.

Paula took a long sip of her tea, then put her glass down. "So much has happened since we've seen each other. We used to be so close..." She pressed a palm to her chest and shook her head.

"I know," Grace whispered, a dull heaviness in her stomach.

"We had some good times together though, didn't we? Over the years? Even the summer you came to visit me in San Francisco?" The half-formed questions flew out of Paula's mouth in a hurried muddle of words.

Grace dipped her head in a perfunctory nod. "Mm-hmm."

"Do you ever think about what happened that night, Gracie?"

Grace dropped her hands into her lap, clasping them together into a single tight-fisted knot. Her shoulders hunched forward, and the air around her grew cold. "I try not to," she said. An honest answer. She swallowed her own question. *Why are you asking me that...now?*

"Well, I do," Paula said. "Sometimes, usually at night when I can't sleep, I replay it in my mind. I try to figure out exactly what happened. I have an idea, but..." Her eyes locked with Grace's. "Did you ever tell anybody?"

Grace inhaled, then opened her mouth and let her breath out in a long, drawn-out stream. "No, I didn't."

"Not even Doug?" Paula asked in a theatrical whisper, her eyes open artificially wide.

Grace pressed her lips together and shook her head. What was going on?

Paula traced the edge of her plate with a finger, her eyes fixed on Grace's face.

Grace lowered her gaze and stared down at the chipped purple polish decorating Paula's fingernails.

"Did you ever think that maybe...?" Paula's words trailed off, leaving the unfinished question dangling.

Grace looked up, chin raised, and met Paula's eyes. "Maybe what, Paula?"

"I never told you what happened to *me* that night." Paula leaned back in her chair, her blue eyes icy. "Did I, Gracie?"

"N-no."

"Well, you see, I got pregnant. Just like you did. But in my case——"

"Wait a minute, Paula." Grace slammed her palm down on the table. "I got pregnant from Doug right before I came to California. I just didn't know it 'til I got back home."

"Okay, okay." Paula raised her hands in surrender. "Anyway, *I* got pregnant that night."

"Are you serious?"

Paula cleared her throat and swallowed. "Oh yes, I'm serious alright. I got pregnant, and I had an abortion done by a shady doctor. Then, when I did want a baby, I wasn't able to have one."

"Oh Paula..." Grace shook her head. "I'm so sorry. I didn't——"

"No, of course you didn't know. I didn't tell anyone about that part." Paula reached for her glass and took a noisy gulp of tea. "But you didn't ask me what I thought you would." Her lips curved into an unsettling close-mouthed smile.

"What's that?"

"Don't you want to know if *I* ever told anyone?" Paula smirked.

"Did you?" Grace's right eyelid began to pulse with a tiny twitch.

"Not at first. But a couple of years later, after the story

hit...about Manson..." Paula's voice lowered to a whisper. "I did tell some of the people I was hanging out with back then."

Grace's mouth fell open, and an invasion of goosebumps attacked her arms. "You did? Why?"

"I don't know. In those days, the people I was spending time with...you know...I guess it seemed kind of...cool? Exciting maybe?" Paula pulled the corner of her bottom lip into her mouth.

Grace slid her hands off the table and curled them into fists against her thighs, digging her nails into her palms. "And what did they say?" she asked, forcing her words to come out smoothly.

Paula chuckled. "No one believed me." Her penciled eyebrows lifted in twin arches. "I mean, after all, I was pretty high all the time back then. I wasn't exactly known for being totally in touch with reality. That was *then* though. You know what I mean?" she said, not waiting for Grace to answer. "I haven't talked about it in a long time, Gracie. But something *did* happen, and it happened to *both* of us."

Grace, her face an expressionless mask, blinked once and stared at Paula. She kept her body rigid, an unmoving statue, as a wave of nausea ripped through her.

"But you were the lucky one. Marriage, a child, and even a grandchild." Paula popped the last bit of her sandwich into her mouth.

Grace ran her hands up and down her thighs, waiting. In what seemed like slow motion, Paula chewed, swallowed, and patted her mouth with a napkin.

"And Doug really built up his family's hardware store. I give him credit for that. You guys owned the property too, right?" Paula plowed on, not needing Grace to give her the answer she already seemed to know. "You must have gotten quite a pretty penny when you sold it, huh?"

An icy tingle darted up Grace's spine. "How do you know all of this, Paula?"

"We might not have kept in touch, Gracie, but I never forgot about you. I never stopped caring about you. And besides, these days everything's on the internet." She paused, her mouth twisting into an ugly smile. "So, in case you were wondering, you didn't have to show me the pictures of Joanna." She chuckled. "I already saw them."

Grace's head bobbed in a mechanical nod.

"Well, like I said, I haven't talked about it in a long time, and I guess you haven't either." Paula leaned back in her chair and looked up at the ceiling. "And it would be a pity if, after all these years, your family found out that..." She lowered her head and looked straight at Grace, her eyes hard, flat pebbles.

Grace clamped her quivering hands onto the edges of her chair. Still, they quivered. "What is it that you want, Paula?"

"I need your help, old friend." She cleared her throat and swallowed, then continued on. "It's just that I'm a little short on my rent this month, and my brother's already bailed me out before. A few times, actually. And I don't want to ask him again." She smacked her lips together, the sound like the pop of a BB gun. "So, I need a loan. Not a gift, Gracie. A loan. I'll pay you back when I can. Okay?"

Okay? As if it was a question...

"Are you kidding me, Paula?" Grace's words came out in a ragged gasp.

"No, Gracie. Unfortunately, I'm not kidding you."

"You can't prove--"

"I'm not the one who would need proof, or who would

even want proof. That would be up to Dawn." Paula shrugged. "There are lots of ways to investigate ancestry these days. You know, she could––"

The sharp, cutting reality of her request––no, her demand––lodged like a jagged rock in Grace's chest. "How much, Paula?"

And just like that, Grace's former best friend, fellow victim of their long-ago mutual mistake, became her blackmailer.

Grace agreed to send Paula a check for two thousand dollars––"a loan, Gracie, just a loan," she promised––and the two women said good-bye with a business-like handshake.

Paula headed toward the street, and Grace ran into the bathroom where she washed her hands in the hottest water she could stand.

She took the escalator up to the next level, and boarding an Oakdale-bound bus, she showed the driver her ticket and claimed an empty seat toward the front. Her head throbbed, and her mouth tasted of sour milk. The bus started to move, and her cell phone rang.

Dawn's name lit up the screen. Grace silenced her phone and let the call go to voicemail.

PART III

19

Dawn finished putting her groceries away and grabbed her cell phone from the counter. Pulling up her recent calls, she tapped "Mom."

Beeeep. Beeeep. Beeeep. Beeeep.

"Hello? Dawn?" Grace answered, her voice muffled and dim as if floating up through a fog.

"I called you before. Didn't you get my message?"

"Um...yes, I did. I was going to call you back in a few minutes. I just got up from a nap."

"A nap? You?"

"I had a headache before," Grace said, her voice growing stronger. "But I'm fine now."

"I tried to call you a couple of hours ago. How long were you sleeping?"

"I don't know. A while, I guess."

"And you didn't hear the phone?"

"I guess not."

"That's not like you, Mom. Are you okay?"

"I'm fine, Dawn. Just tired. That's all."

"You sure? You don't sound like yourself."

"Dawn, I'm fine. Really," Grace said. "But listen, I'm glad you called because I do have to tell you something. It's about Quinn." She paused. "And Paige."

"O-kay." Dawn pressed the phone tighter to her ear.

"Joanna told me that Paige is sleeping over at Quinn's tonight."

"What?" Dawn yelped. "Are you kidding?" she asked, although she already knew the answer. *That* was not something her mother would kid about.

"No, I'm not."

"How did you find out? Did Joanna just come out and tell you? Was she upset?" The questions tumbled out of Dawn's mouth.

"I guess I found out by accident," Grace said. "I asked her what she was doing tonight, and she told me about Ryan's party. Then I asked her if 'the three musketeers' were going too. That's when she told me about the sleepover. But was she upset?" she repeated Dawn's question. "I don't know for sure, but...yes..." Her sigh came through the phone. "I think she might have been. So I was thinking––"

"That it might be time to tell her about Quinn?" Dawn completed her mother's thought.

"I don't know. Maybe."

"I don't know either. Let me think about it," Dawn said. "But thank you, Mom. Thank you for letting me know."

Dawn said good-bye, anxious to end the conversation. She needed to think. She slid a chair back from the kitchen table, and her body went limp as she collapsed into it.

Paige sleeping at Quinn's house? One of her daughter's best friends at the home of a teenage arsonist? Dawn didn't know what to do or even whether to do anything at all. She could call Paige's mother. That was certainly an option. She knew Janice, although not well. But what would she say?

Your daughter is becoming friendly with a girl who was expelled from school for setting fire to a teacher's car?

Dawn felt her jaw tighten, and she shook her head. No. She didn't want to be *that* mother––the busybody, the rumormonger, the gossip. Plus, it wouldn't be fair to Quinn. What if she really was trying to get herself on the right track, to start over? No, calling Janice was not an option.

Dawn's only concern was for her own daughter. And Joanna didn't like Quinn. In fact, she actively *dis*liked her. But what if she changed her mind? What if Paige got Joanna's other friends involved with Quinn? What if Joanna followed them? What if? What if? What if?

Her mother was right. It was time to tell Joanna.

"Come in," Joanna called, answering her mother's knock on her bedroom door.

Dawn stepped inside and entered her daughter's world. Posters of Jimi Hendrix, Santana, and Jefferson Airplane decorated her walls, and tie-dyed scarves and beaded necklaces cascaded over the edges of her dresser mirror. The smell of sandalwood incense hung in the air.

Sitting cross-legged on the bed, Joanna looked up from her open jewelry box. With a toss of her hand, she flipped her hair over her shoulders and held a silvery hoop to one ear and a turquoise drop to the other.

"What do you think?" she asked.

"Hmm..." Dawn tilted her head, first to one side, then to the other. "I really don't know," she said. "One of each?" She smiled.

Joanna laughed and shook her head. "Thanks for your

help, Mom." She pitched the turquoise earring into her jewelry box and slid the silver hoop into her ear.

Settling herself on the edge of the bed, Dawn watched her daughter sift through the jumble of jewelry stashed in her carved wooden box. Joanna dug through the motley assortment of silvery pieces decorated with beads, feathers, and strips of leather. When her fingers finally discovered the mate to her chosen earring, she plucked it out and pushed it through the hole in her other ear.

Joanna was Dawn's dark-haired, blazing-eyed gypsy daughter. Independent and one-of-a-kind. Dawn needed to protect her. She needed to tell her.

"Are you sure you don't want Dad to pick you up from the party tonight?" she asked.

"No, that's alright. Megan's sister can drive us home. She'll be passing right by Ryan's on her way back from another party," Joanna said. "Thanks though."

"No problem. Anytime. And your friends can sleep over, like usual. Just tell me who's coming." Dawn kept her voice even, her face a blank.

Joanna stared down into her jewelry box. "Just Erin and Megan tonight," she mumbled.

"Not Paige?"

"Nope." Joanna snapped the box closed. Springing off the bed, she carried it to the dresser.

"O-kay?" Dawn said, the word a question. A question she already knew the answer to.

Joanna turned to face her mother, her hips against the dresser, her hands gripping its edge. "She's sleeping over at Quinn's."

"Quinn's?" Dawn let her mouth fall open and raised her eyebrows in a mask of surprise. "Are they friends?" she asked, clearing a path to the conversation she wanted to have.

"Who knows?" Joanna shrugged.

Keeping her eyes on her daughter, Dawn ran her tongue over her lips, waiting for her to say more. It didn't take long.

"It's hard to explain, Mom," Joanna began. "It's like Quinn is trying to get into my group. She's starting with Paige, trying to show off how cool she is," she said, shaking her head. "But it's more than that. She wants to be the leader, the one in charge." She stepped away from the dresser and clapped her hands to her thighs, curling them into white-knuckled fists. "And *that*," she spit out the words, "is not going to happen."

Joanna clearly had no desire to pursue a friendship with Quinn. At least Dawn didn't have to worry about that. But what she did have to worry about was her daughter's potential loss of her own friends as, one by one, they fell under Quinn's spell.

Dawn knew what she had to do.

She folded her hands in her lap and leaned forward. "Joanna, I need to tell you something," she said. "Something about Quinn."

Joanna's head tilted. Her eyes narrowed. "You need to tell me something about Quinn?"

"Yes, I do." Dawn nodded. "Joanna, she didn't leave the Tinsley Academy voluntarily." Her mouth went dry, and she bit down on her lower lip, clearing her throat. She swallowed and continued. "She was asked to."

Joanna's eyes flashed with a quick sparkle. "What?" she said, her voice calm, her face unreadable. "Why?"

Dawn sighed, hoping she was doing the right thing by sharing Quinn's story with Joanna. Her daughter should know.

Shouldn't she? She breathed in and then out, feeling her chest rise and fall, and lifted a hand to the back of her neck. Moving her fingers in small circles, she massaged her tense muscles. Now that Quinn was developing a relationship with Paige and maybe even with Joanna's other friends, her daughter needed to know the truth. And it was up to Dawn to tell her. Dropping her hands to her lap, she knit her fingers together as if in prayer.

Opening her mouth, she pushed the words out. "Quinn found out that her mother was having an affair with a teacher at the school, and she set fire to his car. The administrators hushed everything up, but they did ask her to leave, and her parents managed to get her enrolled at Oakdale."

"Seriously?" Joanna gasped.

"Seriously," Dawn said. "But you can't tell anyone, Joanna. Please." She reached for her daughter's wrist. "I don't want you to start a rumor."

"A rumor? But it's true, right?"

"Oh, it's true, Joanna. It's definitely true."

"I won't tell anyone, Mom. I promise." Joanna slid her wrist from her mother's grasp and leaned back. She lowered her eyebrows and blinked. "But why is she here? At Oakdale?"

"Because they live here. In fact, if she hadn't gone to private school all her life, she would have grown up with you," Dawn said. "And your friends."

"But why wasn't she sent to juvie or something? Didn't the police do anything?"

"I don't think they had any solid evidence, although it was an open secret that she was the one who did it," Dawn said. "Besides, it was certainly in the best interests of Quinn's family as well as the school to make it all go away."

Joanna crossed her arms over her chest and rocked back on her heels. "How do you know all this?"

"I recognized her last name, 'Chandler', from a story Lisa had told me a few weeks ago. It happened at Chloe's school. So, when you told me Quinn was in a couple of classes with you, I called Lisa," Dawn said. "She's the same girl, Joanna. Quinn Chandler."

"But I searched for her online. There was nothing anywhere." Joanna's shoulders darted up to her ears, and she lifted her hands, palms up.

"Her name is 'Elizabeth'. 'Quinn' is her middle name. And after everything that happened, she might have just deleted all her social media accounts. So, you wouldn't have found anything anyway."

Joanna's head bobbed up and then down in a slow nod. "Makes sense."

"Yeah, it does."

"But then..." Her forehead wrinkled, and she stepped forward. "Why didn't you tell me any of this before?"

"I don't know." Dawn shook head and looked up at the ceiling, but the answer wasn't there. She lowered her head to meet her daughter's questioning stare. "I guess I thought if the girl wanted to start over, she deserved a chance, and I didn't want to be the one to sabotage her by spreading gossip," she said. "Besides, you didn't like her, so I wasn't worried about you becoming involved with her."

"But now that Paige is sleeping at—"

"Yes, now that Paige seems to be developing some sort of relationship with Quinn, and based on what you've said about her trying to join your group of friends, I decided that I did need to tell you. Do you understand?" Dawn said, ending with the question that *she* needed answered.

Joanna nodded. "I do, and it's okay." She moved toward her mother and kissed her cheek. A quick peck. "Don't worry."

Dawn pulled her daughter into a hug, and Joanna gave her mother's shoulder a hurried squeeze. Then, gracefully disentangling herself from Dawn's arms, she took a step back, turned, and grabbed her cell phone from the night table.

"Mom, I'm sorry, but I have to work out the times for tonight with Erin and Megan," she said, her finger poised above the phone's screen.

"Go ahead, hon. No problem," Dawn said and moved to the door. As she reached for the knob, she turned back toward her daughter. "And Joanna..."

"Huh?" Joanna looked up from her phone.

"Remember not to––"

"I know, Mom." Joanna rolled her eyes. "I won't tell anyone. I said I wouldn't, and I won't," she said. "But thanks for telling *me*." She lifted her arm and raised her thumb, curling her fingers into her palm.

Dawn smiled, returned Joanna's thumbs up, and stepped into the hall. She had done the right thing by telling her. At this point, her daughter did need to know. She hurried down the stairs and into the kitchen.

Mission accomplished. Time to start dinner.

After her mother left, Joanna tossed her phone onto the bed and plopped down next to it, leaning back against her pillows. So, that was the truth about Quinn. Joanna knew something was up with that girl. She had to have more of a backstory than she'd let on. And now, courtesy of her mother, Joanna knew what it was. *Thanks, Mom!* She blew a kiss to her closed door. She wished her mother had told her earlier, but that was her mom. Always trying to do what she thought would be "the right thing." It didn't matter though because ultimately, she had given Joanna the information she wasn't able to dig up on her own.

Joanna scurried across the room, snatched her laptop from the desk, and carried it back to the bed. Perching on its edge, she balanced the computer across her knees and flipped it open. The cursor blinked in the search bar, and her pulse quickened as her fingers flew to the keyboard.

Elizabeth Quinn Chandler

Nothing.

Elizabeth Chandler

A real estate agent, a wedding photographer, a holistic massage therapist, and an aeronautical engineer. Not her girl.

She tried *Elizabeth Chandler* coupled with *Tinsley Academy*, then *New York*, then *New Jersey*, then *fire*. Still nada.

Next, she typed *Tinsley Academy fire*.

Bingo!

Although arson is suspected, no charges have been filed in connection with the car fire that occurred on the grounds of the Tinsley Academy, a private school in Manhattan. Campus police responded to the report of a motor vehicle fire and found the scorched car. Investigators determined that the fire had been set with a gasoline-soaked newspaper thrown into the vehicle. The perpetrator remains unknown at this time. No injuries have been reported.

Woo-hoo! That was the information, including just enough

detail, that Joanna needed. Now, it would simply be a matter of deciding how to use it.

This was going to be fun!

But for tonight, she needed to get herself, along with Erin and Megan, over to Ryan's party.

20

Megan's mother stopped the car in front of Ryan's house, and the three girls jumped out. Joanna marched up the driveway with Megan and Erin following closely behind. They climbed the steps to the door, and Joanna turned to look at her girls.

The V-neck of Megan's shirt dipped just enough to display a hint of her ample cleavage, and her jeans fit well for a change. Erin wore a denim shirt layered over a black tank top and leggings. Her silver hoop earrings were slightly smaller versions of Joanna's.

They were trying, and that was a good sign.

Joanna tilted her head and nodded. "You guys look nice."

Megan smiled, her cheeks turning pink, and Erin mumbled a whispered "thanks."

Joanna reached out and rang the bell. They waited. She knocked. Again, they waited. Finally, Joanna banged on the door, stinging the heel of her right hand, and pushed her left index finger into the bell. This time the door swung open, and a tall guy with spiky dark hair peered down at them, his eyes glassy.

"Hi, we're Ryan's friends," Joanna said.

"Hey, ladies. I'm Zach." His voice was thick, and he stumbled as he took a step backward. "Come on in," he said, sweeping a limp arm through the air behind him.

Megan turned to wave her mother on, and the girls followed Zach inside. The entryway buzzed with the sound of music overlaid with voices and laughter wafting up from below.

"Everyone's in the basement. I was just upstairs to use the...uh...facilities." He smirked. "Most people come in through the back. Good thing I heard you." He turned on his heel, his body swaying drunkenly. "Follow me," he said, heading toward the basement steps.

The boisterous fusion of music mixed with human voices got louder as they walked single file down the narrow stairway, making their way to a closed wood paneled door. Zach pushed the door open with a sneakered foot, and they followed him into the basement.

A crew of familiar-from-school kids surrounded a long rectangular table. Ryan, a ping pong ball in his hand, stood in front of a triangular arrangement of red plastic cups, eyeing its mirror image positioned at the opposite end of the table.

Moving past Zach and motioning Megan and Erin to follow, Joanna strode into Ryan's line of vision and smiled. Ryan met her eyes and nodded, his mouth curving into a wide grin.

"Cover for me, Brett," he said, tossing the ball to his beer pong partner and heading toward her. "Joanna, you came." He cocked his head and squeezed her shoulder.

"I told you I would. I brought Megan and Erin too," Joanna said, glancing back at them.

Megan pulled a fingernail, mid-chew, out of her mouth, and Erin managed a weak smile and a muffled "hi."

"Hey guys, glad you could come," Ryan said, lifting his hand in a wave.

Polite to her girls. A good way to start the night.

"Where's your other friend?" Ryan asked. "Quinn?"

Maybe not so good after all.

Joanna's shoulders tightened, but she forced them up in a nonchalant shrug. "Don't know." She tilted her head and touched the tip of his shoe with toe of her own. "Why? Aren't we good enough for you?"

"You know you are." Ryan lifted his shoe, waggling Joanna's foot, and chuckled. "Now, come on. Let me introduce you." He cupped her elbow and steered her toward the beer pong table.

Joanna turned and glanced back, tugging at Megan's hand and nodding at Erin in a follow-me signal. The girls shaped their mouths into stiff smiles and walked silently behind Joanna.

"Hey guys, this is Joanna," Ryan announced, his hand still gripping her elbow. "And Megan and Ellen."

"*Erin*. Her name is 'Erin', Ryan," Joanna said, jerking her arm away and shooting him a stony glare. "Not 'Ellen'."

"Sorry," he said, tossing his head in Erin's direction.

"S'okay," she mumbled.

"Anyway, this is Brett, Matt, Dan, Emily, Sarah." The names tripped off his tongue as he pointed to each of his friends in turn. "And you met Zach at the door." He cocked his head toward the couch where Zach now sat, his eyes closed and his mouth open. "Guess he started the party a little early." Ryan laughed. "Speaking of which..."

He turned and crossed the room, stopping in front of a mini-fridge. He reached inside and pulled out three cans of beer. "You girls have some catching up to do," he said, handing them each a can. "That is unless you want to join us in beer pong." He smiled and grabbed one of the beer-filled cups from the table, raising it in a mock salute.

"That's okay," Joanna said, shaking her head and speaking for all of them. "Thanks though."

"Then at least stand by me and be my lucky charm." Ryan slipped an arm around her waist and steered her to the edge of the table.

The girls watched as Ryan slowly pulled his arm back and lobbed the little white ball in a graceful arc. Its path curved over the table and ended with a splash in one of the other side's red plastic cups.

"Looks like you gotta drink, buddy," Ryan called out, pointing a finger at Matt. Then bending to kiss Joanna's cheek, he whispered, "Must be my lucky night, babe."

Maybe in beer pong, Joanna thought, swallowing the words she wanted to say.

And don't call me "babe." She didn't say that either.

Matt chugged the beer, and the game continued. Players stepped in and out, exchanged places, and switched sides. The ball was tossed, pitched, thrown, and flung overhand, underhand, and straight across. A raucous cacophony of laughter, cheering, and cursing underscored by the bass-heavy soundtrack of dance music filled the room.

Ryan reached for Joanna's hand, opened it, placed the ping pong ball inside, and closed her fingers around it. "Your turn, girl."

Joanna stole a sidelong glance at her girls. Megan's mouth was open mid-yawn, and Erin's eyes were heavy-lidded. Would they have had a better time with Paige at

Quinn's house? Joanna didn't know if that question had occurred to them. Yet.

She grabbed Erin's hand and pressed the ball into it. Erin stood motionless, holding the ball in her open palm. Joanna stepped back and with her hand under Erin's elbow, nudged her forward to a place at the table.

"I'm not too good at this," she said to Ryan. "Let Erin try." She positioned herself next to Megan, linking their arms together.

Ryan looked at Joanna and raised his eyebrows. Clicking her tongue, she offered him a lopsided smile.

"Okay then," he said, turning back to Erin. "Go ahead. Give it a shot."

Erin looked down at the ball in her hand and slowly lifted and lowered it. Then her eyes moved to the triangle of cups set up across the table. Squinting, she pressed her lips together and stuck her chin out, the same face she made when she was bent over a history test in Mrs. Bergstrom's class. Her jaw tightened, and Joanna watched as she assessed her options.

Underhand or overhand? High arc or straight shot? Gentle toss or fast throw?

Erin wanted to get the ball into one of those cups. Joanna could see the desire and determination on her face. She wanted it badly. And Joanna wanted the night to be successful for Erin and Megan. That's what she wanted. Badly.

Erin brought the ball up to eyebrow level and pulled her hand back.

Make the shot, Erin. Make the shot. Joanna closed her eyes and clamped her hands to her sides.

Make. The. Shot.

The ball hit the table with a sharp tap, and Joanna

opened her eyes. On the opposite side of the table, a smiling Matt watched as the ball dropped onto the floor. Erin stepped back, positioning herself behind Joanna and next to Megan. Matt took aim and threw the ball, missing the cups on Ryan's side.

"Anybody else want to try?" Ryan looked at Joanna.

"Okay, I'll take a shot," she said.

Joanna took the ball, leaned forward, and eyed the table, scrunching her face into a look of concentration. She tossed the ball across the table in a gentle arc calculated to miss. Tap. Tap. The ball hit the table twice and rolled off. She glanced back at Erin, raised her eyebrows, and shrugged.

"It's tougher than it looks," she said, shaking her head and crossing her arms over her chest.

Megan and Erin nodded, their eyes trained on the floor. A silent, unhappy pair. They were her girls, part of her team. Her family. And Joanna needed to make sure they knew it. But bringing them here ––to Ryan's house stocked with beer and his popular, older-than-they-were friends––might have been a mistake. A big one.

A few more rounds, and beer pong was over. The music had gotten lower, and the lights had dimmed. Emily and Dan were making out on a couch in the corner while Zach threw up into a garbage can. Matt had one hand in a bowl of chips and the other pressed against Sarah's back. Megan and Erin had disappeared upstairs. Probably locked away in the bathroom.

Ryan pulled gently on the twin tassels dangling from Joanna's peasant shirt. "C'mon, babe. I want to show you something." He grabbed her hand.

Here we go.

Joanna knew this would happen. Ryan wanted to *show* her something. She looked down at her watch. Another half hour until Megan's sister would come to pick them up. She could think of worse ways to pass the time. Ryan was cute. Hot, actually. He had the floppy hair of a younger Brad Pitt and a quick smile made even more irresistible by the single crooked bottom tooth that saved it from orthodontic perfection. Yeah, ordinarily Joanna wouldn't have had a problem with Ryan. But at that particular moment, she wasn't in a very obliging sort of mood.

The evening hadn't gone at all according to plan. Erin and Megan, instead of reveling in their presence at a gathering of high school royalty, had chosen to hide in anonymity upstairs. Maybe Joanna should have coached them, trained them, prepared them. They were who they were, but she could have made them better.

She could open doors for them, and they knew it. Paige knew it too, although at least for tonight, she had turned her back on their little group, *Joanna's* group. She'd allowed herself to be seduced by the latest bright, new, shiny thing.

And that "thing" was named "Quinn."

But all that glittered wasn't gold, and Quinn's cool girl swagger was a thin disguise for what lay beneath. Something secret, twisted, and dangerous.

Joanna smiled at Ryan. Just a whisper in his ear, a few words to him or to anyone actually, and the gossipy truth of what had happened––and *why*––to a single teacher's car in a private school parking lot would spread like an out-of-control wildfire. Quinn would be melted down and consumed, leaving only a white-haired shadow in her place at Joanna's lunch table and in her life. The ghostly image flickered before her eyes, and then *poof!*––it was gone.

But no, maybe there was a better way. A surer way.

Joanna opened her eyes wide and parted her lips,

donning a mask of sweet innocence. "Okay," she said to Ryan and followed him into his basement storage room.

Kissing, touching, rubbing, and stroking. The typical routine for a high school get-together in a home with absentee parents. It was pleasant enough. Joanna gave Ryan twenty minutes, and then she disentangled herself, buttoned her shirt, smoothed her hair, and rejoined her girls upstairs.

Megan's phone lit up with a text from her sister, and the three girls headed out to her waiting car. Joanna and Erin piled into the back, and Megan slid into the front seat.

"Thanks for picking us up, Dana," Megan said.

"Well, I hope you guys had a good time because Mom made me cut *my* night short in order to come get you," she muttered and pulled away from the curb.

"We appreciate that, Dana," Joanna said.

"Yeah, we do. Thanks, Dana," Erin chimed in.

"So, how was the party?"

Dana's question hung in the air a beat too long. Joanna cleared her throat and opened her mouth, but Megan spoke first.

"G-good. It was good," she said and reached over to turn up the volume on the radio.

Joanna's house was the first stop, and with a quick "thanks" and a "bye, guys," she hurried out of the car.

Dawn heard the front door open and the alarm system chirp

as the code was punched in. Joanna's footsteps echoed in the hall and grew louder as she made her way up the stairs.

The bedside clock's green light glowed in her dark bedroom. 11:50 P.M. Not that late. She slipped out of bed and met her daughter in the hallway.

"How was the party?"

Joanna's hand jumped to her chest. "What are you doing up?"

"I'm a light sleeper. You know that. Guess it's a 'Mom' thing." Dawn laughed. "So, how was it?"

"Good." Joanna yawned. "Fun. I'm really tired though." She yawned again.

"Okay, hon." Dawn kissed her daughter's cheek. "Go to sleep. I'll see you in the morning."

She watched Joanna walk down the hall and into her room. Careful not to wake her gently snoring husband, Dawn crawled back into bed, snuggled next to him, and closed her eyes.

But sleep didn't come easily.

She knew when her daughter's yawn was real. And she knew when it wasn't.

21

Joanna knew her mother suspected that something was up. She hadn't wanted to talk when she came home from Ryan's party. That in itself wasn't especially unusual. But she'd slept late the next morning and missed her mother's blueberry pancakes. *That* was unusual. Plus, she was sullen and kind of pouty when she finally did get out of bed. She made the excuse that she had a lot of homework and an English paper due. But she'd caught her mother staring at her with that intense look she got when she was worried about something.

She'd need to be extra careful.

She stared at the blank screen on her laptop, but she couldn't concentrate on "The Use of Stereotypes in *Lord of the Flies*." Closing her computer, she snatched up her cell phone. She leaned back in her desk chair, tapped the voice-mail icon, and for the third time, listened to Paige's bubbly message.

"Hey, Joanna. Call me back, okay? Erin told me about Ryan's party, but I wanna tell you about last night. So, call me, 'kay?"

Might as well get it over with. Joanna sighed and touched her finger to Paige's name.

She answered on the first ring. "Hey, Joanna."

"Hi, Paige," Joanna said and waited for Paige to speak.

"So," she began. "Erin told me about Ryan's party. She said *you* had a good time."

"It was good," Joanna said lightly.

"So, you and Ryan? Are you...uh...together?"

"It's not a big deal, Paige," Joanna said. "How was your night at Quinn's?"

She hated to ask that question, but she didn't want to talk about Ryan or his party. And she certainly didn't want to talk about Erin and Megan. Anyway, that was all it took, and off Paige went, spewing out words at breakneck speed.

Yak, yak, yak...Paige was still talking. Joanna flipped her laptop open to check the time. Fifteen painful minutes had crept by, and she was still listening to Paige go on and on about her night at Quinn's.

Amazing. Awesome. The best night ever.

Joanna heard about Quinn's cool mom who let her daughter help herself to the liquor cabinet and understood when she asked for the occasional mental health day off from school. She heard about the older dad––"a little nerdy, but nice"––who didn't mind when his much younger wife went out dancing with her girlfriends "to blow off some steam."

"And you gotta see the car they drive. A red Porsche convertible. It's vintage, like from the nineties or something, and it's a two seater. I mean, they have a family car too. But that's what they drive when it's just the two of them."

Joanna didn't respond. She didn't have to. Paige was on a roll. Her next topic was Quinn's older brother, Derek, a student at NYU.

"Quinn put me on the phone with him," Paige said.

"You spoke to him?" Joanna asked, regretting the question as soon as the words popped out of her mouth.

It wasn't as if she cared...

"I did." Paige said. "After a couple of vodka shots." She giggled. "And the next time he's home from school, Quinn wants to invite all of us over."

"*All* of us?" Joanna asked, keeping her voice calm.

"Yeah, you know––you, me, Erin, and Megan." Paige's voice dropped to a fluttery whisper. "She might even get Derek to invite some of his friends."

Erin and Megan with Derek's friends? College guys? They couldn't even handle high school boys. And Paige wouldn't be able to either. Was she out of her mind?

"Okay. We'll see," Joanna said and cleared her throat, a signal for a topic change. "Paige?"

"Yeah?"

"Did Quinn ever tell you why she left her school in New York?"

Paige's irritated groan was loud enough for Joanna to hear through the phone. "She already told us, Joanna. She *lives* in Oakdale, and she wanted the experience of going to a public school."

"But why didn't she start at the beginning of the school year instead of waiting 'til October?"

"She told us that too. She had to convince her parents." Paige spit the words out rapid fire. Rat-a-tat-tat.

"Okay," Joanna said and smoothly moved their conversation to Paige's usual favorite topics––homework, clothes, and TV––until she was able to say good-bye.

The echo of Paige's voice, high-pitched and giddy, rico-cheted through Joanna's brain like a pinball in motion. She knew Paige. She knew what she wanted, she knew how she thought, and she knew that the undercurrent of caution beneath her zippy account of her night with Quinn was real.

Paige still couldn't say the words she'd been swallowing for the past few months. *I don't need you anymore, Joanna.* She wasn't ready. Not yet. But her huffy response to questions about Quinn told Joanna that she would be soon.

And *that* was Quinn's fault.

A wintry chill, emanating from deep within Joanna's chest, coursed through her. The back of her neck felt prickly and cold, and her breath came out in sharp, raggedy blasts.

She needed to come up with a plan, and she needed to do it quickly.

22

With her elbows planted on the kitchen table and a pen clasped between her fingers, Grace's hand hovered above the blank check marked with her name and address. The long horizontal line following the words "Pay to the Order of" taunted her.

Yes, that was exactly what she would be doing––paying to Paula's *order*. She pressed her lips together, tightened her grip on the pen, and printed her former friend's name.

Paula Milgram.

The black handwritten letters stood stark against the pale yellow background of the check. She filled in the amount––*Two thousand dollars and 00/100*––and the date, scribbled her signature, and copied the address Paula had given her onto a generic white envelope. She stamped the envelope, folded the check in half, and slid it inside.

She stared at Paula's name, printed in her own hand, on the envelope. When was the last time she had written it? After Paula and her family moved to San Francisco, the girls had sent each other long, rambling letters decorated with felt-tipped squiggles and hand-drawn doodles, never deviating from their shared custom of garnishing Paula's last name with a heart-topped *i*. Grace had saved them all.

Pushing back her chair, she snatched up the envelope—the *i* in *Milgram* heart-less—and headed out the door, not bothering with a jacket. Down the steps and across her front lawn, she hurried to the mailbox. Empty. Good, the postman hadn't been there yet. She slid the envelope into the box and raised the red flag. In less than an hour, the check would be in the mail. Literally. And Grace would be done.

She stashed her checkbook in the catch-all drawer under the kitchen counter and made her way up the stairs. Pulling the stack of Paula's letters, tied with a faded blue ribbon, from the bottom drawer of her night table, she carried it back downstairs and into the kitchen. She flipped up the lid of the trash can and dumped the complete handwritten history of their friendship inside.

That Paula no longer existed.

But Grace still had one more thing to do.

Back in her bedroom, she opened her jewelry box. Buried beneath a tangle of silver, turquoise, and painted beads, she pulled out a brown plastic guitar pick and a wrinkled photograph of a Victorian-style row house. She laid the guitar pick on top of the picture and crumpled the whole mess into a crinkly ball.

That place and that night no longer existed either.

23

Dawn stopped at the open door leading to the garage and touched her husband's shoulder. "I just want to ask her one more time."

"Dawn, she already told us––"

"I know, but––"

Tom chuckled and shook his head. "Okay, never mind. Ask her again if you want. I'll meet you in the car."

"I'll just be a minute." Dawn raised a finger and scurried back into the house. "Joanna, are you sure you don't want to come with us?" she called up from the bottom of the staircase.

"I can't, Mom. Too much homework. But have fun," came her answer.

"Okay. Next time then."

Dawn set the alarm, locked the door to the house, and slid into the car next to Tom. He raised his eyebrows, and she shook her head. She buckled her seatbelt, and Tom began to back down the driveway.

"You don't think it's odd that Joanna didn't want to come

with us?" Dawn blurted out the question that had been gnawing at her.

"Why would it be odd?" Tom lifted his shoulders in a quick shrug, his eyes not moving from the road. "She went out last night, and she's got homework and a paper to write."

"I don't know. I think it's more than that," Dawn said, clicking her tongue against the roof of her mouth. "Even last night when I heard her come in, I met her in the hallway. She seemed odd. Evasive. She acted like she was tired, but I could tell she wasn't."

"What do you expect? She's a teenager. She's not going to tell you everything. That's normal."

"Something's bothering her, Tom. I can sense it."

He shot her a sidelong glance. "What could be bothering her?"

"I'm not sure exactly. It's just that she seems...I don't know...Preoccupied? Troubled? Disturbed?" She struggled to pin a word on a mother's intuition for a feeling she didn't quite understand.

"What do you think it is? School? Friends? Boys?" Tom reached out to touch her knee. "A particular boy?"

"No, it's not a *particular* boy." Dawn smiled at her husband's classic father-of-a-teenage-girl response.

"Then what do you think the problem is?"

She pushed her lips together and opened them with a popping sound. "I think it might have something to do with Quinn."

"Quinn? The girl who started the car fire?"

"Uh-huh." She nodded, her eyes widening.

"But Joanna doesn't want anything to do with her, right?" Tom asked. "That's still true, isn't it?" He swiveled his head toward Dawn, his eyes narrowing.

"Yes, yes. That's still true." She thrust a finger at the windshield. "Tom, watch the road."

Tom returned his gaze to the road ahead, his fingers tightening on the steering wheel. "So, what's going on then?"

"Paige slept over at Quinn's house last night instead of going to Ryan's party with Joanna and the other girls."

"Okay...?"

"No, Tom. Not 'okay'. Joanna thinks Quinn is trying to worm her way into her group of friends. And not only that, but she thinks Quinn is trying to steal them away and maybe even become their leader." Dawn's words came out fast and loud, hurt and angry on her daughter's behalf.

"Is Joanna jealous that she wasn't invited to sleep over at Quinn's?"

"No, of course not. But––"

"So, she does *not* want to become Quinn's friend?"

"No, she doesn't. Thank goodness! But if Joanna's friends all start––"

"Dawn, I really think you're jumping to conclusions. Just because Paige spent one night with Quinn doesn't mean she'll throw away her friendship with Joanna. Nor does it mean that the other girls will desert her. Joanna has been friends with all of them for years. They look up to her," Tom said, his voice patient and kind.

"I know..." Dawn sighed, her head dipping in a hesitant nod.

"And I have another question––Were Erin and Megan invited to Quinn's?"

"N-No."

"Okay then," Tom said. "I would be concerned if you'd told me that all three of them, with the *exception* of Joanna, had been invited. And I'd be even more concerned if you'd told me that Joanna was developing a friendship with Quinn. But this?" He tilted his head toward Dawn's and shrugged. The corners of his mouth turned up into the same gentle smile that had made her fall in love with him so many years ago.

Tom was right. Joanna's friends were loyal, and they did look up to her. She was the one who made the plans. The others followed. She was a natural leader, and the arrangement seemed to work for all of them. They wouldn't desert her. Just because Paige had slept over at Quinn's...

Dawn tapped her chin, thinking. No, she didn't want to read more into it than she should. And it wasn't as if Joanna had sat home alone. She'd gone with Erin and Megan to Ryan's party, and she said it was good. That was the word she'd used. "Good."

Dawn hadn't pumped her daughter for more information. Joanna needed her privacy, and she deserved it. So, as long as she didn't pursue a friendship with Quinn, there was nothing to worry about.

They turned onto her mother's street, and Dawn glanced over at her husband and smiled.

With Hendrix on her lap, Grace peered through the slatted wood blind covering her dining room window and watched the street for Tom's car. Her last conversation with Paula replayed in her head like the endless loop of an old 8-track tape. Everything had started out so well. Paula had spoken about her life, and yes, she had made some bad decisions along the way, but she seemed to have pulled herself together. And of course, they'd reminisced, smiling over memories of their shared youth. But then, all of a sudden... Bam! Everything changed.

That must have been Paula's plan all along, and when Grace showed her the pictures of Joanna, she seized on them as even more support for her wacky theory. She fixated on the fact that Joanna didn't look like the rest of Grace's family. Fixated. She refused to let it go. Did she really think that Joanna...? Grace clenched her teeth and shook her head so violently that Hendrix meowed and looked up at her, his golden eyes wide.

"Shhh...it's okay, boy," she whispered and petted the top of his head.

Paula even knew about the hardware store and the property. So, it wouldn't have been hard for her to figure out that Grace was a wealthy woman. She must have had it all planned out—gaining her former friend's sympathy by sharing her sad stories and playing up their connection by trotting out nostalgic memories.

But what if...? Yes, what if...? What if Joanna had been light-haired and green-eyed? No. Grace shook her head again, more gently this time. Pictures of Joanna would have been easy to find on Facebook and whatever other social media the kids, and probably even Dawn, were using these days. Paula must have already known what Joanna looked like. Grace was sure of it.

But Dawn was Doug's child, and Joanna was his granddaughter. Those were the facts. End of story. There was no sense dredging up the past, and if it took a few thousand dollars to buy Paula's silence, so be it. It was money well spent. Grace refused to worry about it anymore.

It was done. Over.

She turned her attention back to the street. The darkening sky was shot through with streaks of orange, the front lawn speckled with red and gold leaves. She'd rake tomorrow and the day after. Maybe the day after that too. No rush. Little by little, she'd uncover the grass, still more green than brown, as it would be for the next month or so. Dawn and Tom wanted to send their landscaper over to do the job, but for Grace, it was a fall tradition. A way of marking the season, acknowledging the passage of time.

Spotting Tom's car from her post at the window, she lifted Hendrix off her lap and ran her hand in a long stroke from his head to his tail. Settling him into her still-warm chair, she tickled the sweet spot under his chin, and his eyes closed. She grabbed her jacket and hurried to the door. Locking it behind her, she dashed down the front steps and ran along the stone path leading to her driveway. The car was already there.

"One of these days I'm going to get out the door before you make it up the driveway," she called out.

Tom poked his head out the window and grinned. "Not as long as I'm driving."

Grace slid into the back seat. "Where's Joanna?" she asked.

Dawn swiveled her head around to face her mother. "She couldn't come. She had homework."

Homework? Joanna was missing a family dinner because of homework? Something didn't sound right. Grace met Dawn's eyes in the rearview mirror. Dawn's brows lifted, and Grace realized that her daughter was just as confused as she was.

"Oh...hmm," Grace said, feeling the corners of her mouth turn down. "That's too bad."

"Guess you'll have to manage with just Dawn and me this time." Tom chuckled.

"Never a problem, Tom. You know that." She reached

forward and squeezed her son-in-law's shoulder. "Just missing my girl."

"Don't worry, Mom. You'll have plenty of time with her when we go away next week," Dawn said. "Unless you change your mind, that is." She laughed.

"Not a chance," Grace said, shaking her head.

24

J oanna and Quinn settled into a school day routine. Each morning Quinn climbed onto what was now *their* bus, strutted down the aisle, and tossed Joanna a fake grin coupled with a mumbled "hi" as she slid into the seat in front of her. Joanna would then lift her hand in a stiff wave and return to her book.

They kept their distance in Mr. Reed's geometry class, and Joanna held back a snide chuckle each time Quinn pulled off her beret in Mrs. B.'s history class, exposing the dark roots lurking beneath her white-blonde hair.

Lunch period was a bit more interesting. Each day Paige tiptoed across a conversational tightrope of her own making, sucking up to Quinn without openly dissing Joanna.

Although all that posturing must have been exhausting for poor little Paige, Joanna's only job was to rein in the smirk that played at the edges of her mouth while she sat back and enjoyed the show. She didn't know if Erin or Megan had picked up on the undercurrents of dislike and distrust swirling around them at their fake wood lunch table, but it didn't matter. It had all seemed to be working.

But now, after Paige's "best night ever" sleepover at Quinn's house coupled with Ryan's disappointing-to-Erin-and-Megan party, Joanna began to feel a barely there shift in the ground that had always been so solid beneath her. Although she was still at the center of her little family, she knew she would have to fight to remain there.

It was about power.

That was what it had always been about.

Power.

Joanna had always had it, and she still did. Most people who knew her would probably assume that the most valuable gifts she had been born with were physical beauty and exceptional intelligence, but they would be wrong. Although those were important attributes, and Joanna had certainly benefited from them, they were not the essential traits that had made her into who she was and who she had become.

The single and most crucial quality that had allowed Joanna to attain her unique power was her unbridled lust to lead, to influence, and to control. That fierce hunger sprang from the essence of her core. It was a primal urge.

And she was not going to let her position and power over the group she'd created be undermined by a white-haired, beret-wearing girl arsonist who had been kicked out of a New York City private school. That was *not* going to happen.

Joanna was a few minutes late for lunch, and the others had already started to eat. Claiming the empty seat next to Quinn, she nodded at her three girls across the table. She was greeted with a quick smile from Megan, a "Hey, Joanna" from Erin, and a lackluster wave from Paige. No one asked why she was late. Megan chomped on her tuna sandwich, her cheeks bulging like a hungry chipmunk's, Erin dipped a spoon into her soup, and Paige leaned forward, ignoring her food, her elbows planted on the table. Her eyes were lined in black, Quinn-style. She must have learned that little trick at their "awesome" and "amazing" sleepover. Maybe a beret and bleached white hair would be next on her agenda.

Megan, Erin, and Paige––all three of them––as if drawn by a single magnet, were focused on Quinn. Joanna followed their collective gaze, and tilting her head and glancing sideways, took stock of her nemesis.

Quinn, the would-be usurper.

Her eyes, more expertly lined than Paige's, were opened wide, and her mouth was in chatter mode. Joanna usually tuned her out, but today she decided to listen and watch as *her* girls allowed themselves to be seduced by Quinn's stories of celebrity sightings and partying in downtown New York clubs with her brother's college friends. Her voice was sexy and throaty in the practiced way of a reality TV star.

"And next time," she said in an exaggerated whisper, "you can come with me." One by one, she locked eyes with Megan, Erin, and Paige. Then, turning to Joanna, she smiled, baring her straight white teeth. "*All* of you."

The table went quiet, and Joanna could feel three pairs of eyes lasering into the side of her head as she angled her body toward Quinn. "Sure," she said, lifting her shoulders in a shrug. "Why not?"

"And hey, if you want," Quinn said, "you can even invite your friend." She jerked her thumb in the direction of Ryan's table. "What's his name again?" She squinched her eyes and tapped her cheek.

What's his name again? She damn well knew Ryan's name. And yes, he was Joanna's friend. Just like everyone else at the table. *Her* table. But two could play Quinn's little game.

"Whose name?" she asked.

"Oh, you know. That guy who comes over to our table sometimes," Quinn said without missing a beat. "Brian? Is that his name?"

That guy who comes over to our table sometimes? He came over to *Joanna's* table, and he did it to flirt with *her*. Quinn knew that. And she knew his name wasn't 'Brian' either.

Joanna clenched her hands in her lap and dug her fingernails into her palms. "No, his name is 'Ryan'," she said.

"Ryan...Brian...whatever." Quinn lifted her shoulders and extended her hands, palms up in a so-what? gesture.

"Yeah, whatever." Joanna mimicked her shoulder lift-hand extension combo.

Whatever? Whatever like 'Quinn'? Or was it 'Elizabeth'? Which name did you go by at your old school? Huh? The questions darted through her brain, but she kept them locked up inside her head. Information was power. And power could be magnified by shrewd timing. Joanna had learned that a long time ago.

She could wait.

"So, I'll let you know the next time I––"

BEEP...BEEP...BEEP...BEEEEEP. Three short blasts and one long one.

"A fire drill? Now?' Megan groaned. "During lunch?" She dropped her half-eaten sandwich onto her napkin, converting it into a soggy package, and tucked it into her backpack.

"That is disgusting," Paige muttered.

Megan's cheeks turned pink. "I didn't finish eating, Paige. And who knows how long––"

BEEP...BEEP...BEEP...BEEEEEP.

"Let's go, everyone. Leave your trays. No running," Ms. What's-Her-Name, the cafeteria monitor, called from the doorway. "Single file."

Slinging their backpacks over their shoulders, the girls joined the line at the door, made their way through the crowded hall, and stepped out into the parking lot and the autumn sunshine.

"At least it's not cold," Erin said, tilting her face up to the sun.

Teachers, pressing their clipboards to their chests, barked instructions.

Everyone, move to your assembly points.

Let's go.

No dawdling.

Talk to your friends later.

Keep moving.

The girls scattered and joined their assigned groups arranged by homeroom. There were a few stragglers, but they all knew the drill and followed the instructions. Joanna's homeroom teacher checked names off his list, leaving his students to wait. Cell phones were pulled out of pockets, purses, and backpacks, and the air filled with the jabbering buzz of bored teenagers trying to pass the time.

Suddenly, a loud voice broke through the hubbub. "Look over there!"

Heads turned, and as a group, the students and teachers watched as a red SUV, emblazoned with gold letters, pulled into the parking lot.

Oakdale Fire Department.

And then they knew. This was not a drill.

The door swung open, and Captain Hill, the smiling fireman Joanna remembered from his visit to her middle school in a gleaming fire truck, stepped out. But this time he wasn't smiling. Using his hand as a makeshift visor, he scanned the snaky rows of students and teachers spread across the parking lot, his mouth pressed into a hard, straight line. Then suddenly, with a quick pivot, he turned on his heel and marched into the school building.

As if on cue, an onslaught of shouted questions flew scattershot through the air.

Why is he here?

What's going on?

Did anyone see smoke?

Is this a real fire?

Even the teachers looked confused, shaking their heads and rubbing their chins. For once, they didn't have the answers.

Mr. Becker, the balding gym teacher with a body shaped like an upside-down pyramid, squawked into a blue megaphone. "All students must remain with their homeroom teachers. No one has permission to leave." He paraded up and down the rows of students, repeating his announcement again and again.

Joanna waited for the dramatic arrival of a bright red fire truck, complete with screaming siren and flashing lights. But it didn't come. Mr. Becker's voice grew thin and hoarse, and he returned to his post at the school's entrance, his megaphone dangling from his hand. No one seemed frightened, just curious and happy to be out of the classroom on a sunny, warm-for-fall day.

Ten more minutes went by, and then the PA system came to life with a staticky crackle. A throat was cleared, and the principal's booming voice bellowed across the parking lot.

"All clear. I repeat––All clear. Students and teachers report to your homerooms. Fifth period will be shortened with a delayed beginning. Please await further instructions. Report to your homerooms immediately."

The parking lot was suddenly transformed into a mass of scattered bodies in motion as students broke free from their assigned homeroom groupings. They had only minutes to find their friends, figure out what had just happened, and report to their homerooms.

"Stay in line. No running!" Mr. Becker yelled into his megaphone, his voice clear and full.

But this time, no one listened.

Joanna lifted her backpack from the ground and hoisted it onto her shoulder. Steering clear of all the people scurrying around her, she made her way across the parking lot in a slow, casual stroll, leaving it to her girls to find her.

And they did.

"Hey, Joanna." Erin was the first to tap her shoulder. "What do you think? Was there a fire?" she asked, hoarsely whispering into Joanna's ear. "A real one?"

Joanna shrugged and raised her eyebrows. "No clue."

"Joanna! Erin!" Paige's voice rang out behind them.

Joanna ignored her and kept walking, leaving it to Paige to catch up.

Erin tugged at Joanna's elbow. "Joanna, Paige is here."

Joanna turned, shot Paige a plastered-on smile, and slowed her pace.

"Did you hear anything?" Paige slid herself between Joanna and Erin.

"No, did you?" Erin said.

Paige shook her head.

Not bothering to answer, Joanna stepped away from Paige, forcing a distance between them, and continued to walk toward the school.

"Hey, wait up, guys!" Megan called out.

And for *her*, Joanna stopped and turned around.

Megan's breath came out fast and hard, and her face was red. Her chest rose and fell, and the gap between the middle two buttons on her shirt did a jiggly dance, playing peek-a-boo with her too-tight bra.

She really should have worn a tank top under that shirt.

"Shouldn't we be going back to fourth period instead of our homerooms?" she asked. "To the cafeteria?"

"What's the matter, Megan? Didn't you get to finish your sandwich?" Paige rolled her eyes. "The one you stuffed in your backpack?"

"I-I was hungry. I didn't have time to eat breakfast today," Megan mumbled, her eyes on the ground.

Paige had a serious mean streak. Joanna had always known that, but it was getting worse.

"Where's Quinn?" she asked, switching the topic to Paige's new BFF.

"Oh, that was weird actually," Megan answered before Paige could speak. "Quinn's in my homeroom, and Mr. Osborne came out and said something to my teacher when we were waiting back there." She pointed toward the parking lot. "Then he walked over to Quinn, and she went back into the school with him."

"Who's 'him'?" Paige asked.

"Mr. Osborne."

"Wait a minute." Joanna stopped, whirled around, and turned to face Megan, her hand held up like a stop sign. "Quinn went into the school with the principal?"

"Uh-huh." Megan nodded.

"Why?" Paige asked, her face close to Megan's.

Megan stepped back. "I don't know." She shook her head.

"I'm sure you'll find out, Paige," Joanna said. "Meanwhile, I need to get to my homeroom." She tossed her head, flipping her hair over her shoulder, and started to walk toward the school building. She didn't look back. She knew her girls would be following.

So, evidently Mr. Osborne wanted to have a word with Quinn. Privately. *Ha!* Joanna's chest felt fluttery as if happy butterflies were dancing inside of her.

Once they were in the building, the girls separated, heading off to their individual homerooms in anticipation of the summons to report to their fifth period classes. But instead, a PA announcement commanded that all students remain in their homerooms and await further instructions.

All at once, everyone was talking. Joanna's homeroom was abuzz with a chaotic chorus of voices, making comments and asking questions.

Hey, this is serious!

Shouldn't they be telling us what's going on?

No complaints here. I'm missing a math test.

Twenty-two heads turned toward the small woman sitting at the large desk at the front of the room. But the way Ms. Coleman rubbed the back of her neck, combined with the paleness of her face, told her students that their teacher was as clueless as they were.

"Please remain in your seats, everyone. I'm sure everything will be explained as soon as information becomes available," she said, sounding like a newscaster caught on camera without any news to report.

Someone near the window groaned, and the rest of the class returned to debating what-if theories until a perfunctory knock on the room's open door stopped the chatter.

Joanna recognized the thin woman with the kind of hair that seemed to grow out rather than down as one of the assistants who worked in the main office. Ms. Coleman waved her in, and the woman stepped over to her desk. Bending her legs into an almost-squat and leaning down, she spoke softly to the teacher.

Ms. Coleman stood, pushing her chair back with a loud scrape, and scanned the room. Her eyes settled on Joanna's face, and she called out her name. "Joanna," she announced. "You are wanted in the office. Please go with Ms. Henderson."

The room stilled into a sudden quiet.

Me? Joanna bit down on the one word question that popped into her mind.

Lifting her backpack by its top loop, she sashayed to the front of the room in a graceful glide, her back straight and head high, and met Ms. Henderson at the door. Neither of them spoke as Joanna followed her down the hallway to the main office. Their footsteps echoed in the empty corridor. Ms. Henderson opened the door to the suite of offices, and walking past the attendance desk, led Joanna into the waiting area outside the principal's office.

Paige, Erin, and Megan, white-knuckled hands clasped in their laps, occupied the first three seats.

"Wait here, Joanna." Ms. Henderson pointed to the empty chair next to Megan. "Mr. Osborne will be with you shortly."

Joanna lowered herself into the chair and leaned over to smile at her girls.

Things were about to get interesting.

25

"So, it was a real fire? Not a drill?" Dawn leaned across the kitchen table, pushing her chest into its edge, her eyes going wide as she stared at her daughter.

"Uh-huh." Joanna pressed her finger into the last cookie crumb on her plate and popped it into her mouth.

"Okay, Joanna. I need you to start from the beginning. Tell me exactly what happened."

"Fine. I'll tell you everything I know. But please calm down. There's nothing for you to worry about. It was just a small fire that started in the girls' room, and it was put out very quickly."

"No one was hurt?"

"No," Joanna said, shaking her head. "No one was hurt."

"Well, that's the most important thing. But go on. Tell me what happened."

Joanna reached for her glass and took a deep swallow of water. "We were at lunch, and the fire alarm went off. Everyone thought it was another one of those drills, and we went outside like we always do. We were out there for a while, but that's normal. No one really thought anything of it until Captain Hill from the fire department drove up."

"Okay…"

"He came in that SUV he drives, not a fire truck. So, we still didn't think it was that big of a deal. Maybe just some kids smoking in the bathroom who set off the alarm." Joanna shrugged. "And that's actually what it was."

"So, it was just smoke then, not a fire?"

"No, Mom." Joanna shook her head. "It was a fire. They told us later that someone must have dropped a cigarette in the trash can in the girls' room, and that's what started it. But the maintenance guys got it under control right away, so there wasn't much damage."

"Do they know who did it?"

"Well…" Joanna patted her mouth with a napkin. "Mr. Osborne brought Quinn into his office for questioning."

"What?"

"Yup," she said, leaning back in her chair, stretching her arms out behind her, obviously savoring the moment.

"Joanna, what happened?" Dawn's voice came out in a hoarse whisper, and she laid her hands down flat on the table, her shoulders hunching forward.

"Well, I got called down to the office, and––"

"*You*?"

"Mom, please."

Dawn clasped her hands together and nodded. "Okay, go on."

"So, I got called down to the office, and Paige, Erin, and Megan were already there. Mr. Osborne spoke to each of us, one at a time, and asked if anyone had left our table during lunch. We all said 'no'. Then, he asked each of us specifically if Quinn had left. And we all said 'no' to that too." Joanna pushed her lips together and opened them with a soft smacking sound. "And Megan told us that Quinn was walking out of Mr. Osborne's when she got there."

"Does he think Quinn did it?"

"I don't know what he thinks."

"Okay then," Dawn said quietly. "Do *you* think Quinn did it?"

"I don't know." Joanna shrugged. "She didn't leave the lunch table when I was there. But then...Could she have stopped into the girls' room for a cigarette before lunch?" She lifted her eyebrows. "I guess she *could* have. But so far, I don't think anyone knows who did it."

"Well, obviously the principal has to be aware of Quinn's ...uh...*past*, and that must be why he singled her out. I suppose it does make sense." Dawn looked down at the table and then raised her eyes to meet her daughter's. "Especially if he suspects the fire was set deliberately."

"Yeah." Joanna nodded. "I guess it does."

"But why would she––?"

"Mom, I have no idea why she does..." Joanna threw her hands in the air. "Anything."

"Okay." Dawn wet her lips and swallowed. "I need you to listen to me, Joanna. I want to make sure you––"

"I know, Mom." Joanna held up a hand. "Keep my distance."

"That's my girl. Keep your distance, Joanna. Please."

After Joanna finished eating, she headed up to her room to do homework––*yeah, right*–– and closed her door, pressing her ear up against it. A minute passed, then two, then three, until she heard her mother's voice. She couldn't make out the beginning of the conversation, but then the voice rose.

"Yes, it had to be Quinn. Who else?"…"They don't know. Not for sure."…"So, what do you think, Mom?"

Mom. That meant she was talking to Grace-ma.

"I have to be honest though. I'm not sure it's a good time for me to go away. I don't want——"

No, no, no. She couldn't cancel her plans. No!

"It's not that, Mom. I know you can——"…"I know he'd be disappointed, but——"…"You're right. But still——"

There was a long pause. Joanna crossed her fingers. C'mon, Mom.

"Okay. Okay. You win," Dawn finally said. "I'll go."

Yes!!!

Poor Quinn. It really wasn't fair. Just because she set one fire didn't mean she'd set another. And to be singled out like that? In front of her whole homeroom? How embarrassing!

Joanna tipped her head back and laughed out loud.

Mr. Osborne had questioned them all——Joanna, Paige, Erin, and Megan. One by one, he had called them into his office. He began with the general questions. *Did you notice anything unusual? Anything at all? Perhaps a smell?* Then, he'd moved on to the specifics. *Did anyone leave your table? Even for a short time? What about Quinn? Are you sure? Think carefully.*

And after that of course, Quinn had faced a barrage of questions from the girls, each of them beginning with a "why." But she'd dealt with everything like a pro, offering up the handy explanation that as "the new girl," she would naturally have been the first one questioned.

Joanna's own girls nodded in easy acquiescence, and Quinn shrugged, flipped her white-blonde hair over her shoulder, and shrugged again, thus closing the door on any possible doubt, disbelief, or additional questions they might have had.

Joanna had to give her credit. The girl was good.

But then again, so was she.

In fact, Joanna was good enough to act just as surprised as everyone else when a seemingly routine fire drill had turned out to be more than just a drill.

And all it had taken was a quick detour to the girls' room before lunch and a tiny cigarette ember tossed into a paper-filled trash can.

So, yes...poor, poor Quinn.

26

"The captain has turned off the *Fasten Seat Belts* sign, and you are now free to move about the cabin. However, we suggest you keep your seat belts fastened while you are seated." The announcement came over the loudspeaker.

"California, here we come," Tom said, touching his head to Dawn's. "You know, this is a long overdue vacation for us." He reached for her hand and squeezed it. "Just you and me."

"Just you and me," Dawn repeated his words and threaded her fingers through his.

"And you know Joanna will be fine, right?"

Tom, the mind reader. Joanna was never far from Dawn's thoughts, and her husband knew it.

"I know." She nodded and smiled at him.

And that was true. Joanna would be fine. She wasn't the kind of kid Dawn had to worry about. An exceptional student, gifted actually, with nice friends. And Dawn knew she could trust her daughter. Joanna was honest, kind, and just all around good. She leaned back against the seat, adjusted her travel pillow, and closed her eyes.

Her vacation with Tom would be good for Joanna, and it would be good for Grace too. Dawn pictured the two of them sitting close together, heads bent over their scrapbook, long hair cascading down their backs—her mother's blonde, these days threaded with gray, and Joanna's shiny and dark. Seeing her own mother as a grandmother, her daughter's Grace-ma—so calm, so at ease—had been a gift for Dawn. A healing gift.

Still, even after so many years, her mother remained an enigma. In lots of ways, she would always be the eighteen-year-old woman-child who wore a wreath of daisies crowning her head and a white flowy dress that skimmed her rounded belly when she married Doug in the church where they'd both attended Sunday school years earlier. The youthful spirit, optimism, and sunny disposition that characterized Grace as a teenager had never left her, not even after she'd been prematurely thrust into adulthood. And it made the lives of her husband, her daughter, and anyone lucky enough to be swept up into her orbit a rollicking and joyous adventure.

To Grace, the act of baking wasn't complete without a flour-splotched floor, and summer showers were a signal to run outside and dance barefoot in the rain. She shared her daughter's belief that wearing pajamas inside out could make it snow and once insisted that Doug pull off the highway so they could all marvel at the appearance of a sudden rainbow. She didn't freak out when Dawn and her friends trailed sandy footprints through the house after a day at the beach or even the time that Dawn had turned one of her bedroom walls into a finger-painted work of art.

Dawn's home was always *the* house—first for play dates, and then later, for sleepovers and boy-girl parties. Grace never told them to lower the music, and she turned a blind eye to the occasional beer can that one of Dawn's friends hadn't buried deep enough within the tall green trash can in the garage. She didn't nag her daughter to do her homework, and she didn't seem to care that Dawn used the chair in her bedroom as a pit stop between her closet and the laundry room for an ever-growing pile of clothing. So yes, Dawn was the girl with the "cool mom," the girl who didn't have to clean her room, the girl without a curfew, the girl whose house was always open.

Lucky Dawn, right?

Her best friend, Lisa, was the only one who knew the truth––the only one who knew that Grace Raymond, the coolest mom in Chester Grove, regularly eavesdropped on her daughter's conversations and searched her room, even finding the last place Dawn had hidden her diary after she'd moved it from the more obvious backpack to an old Barbie doll case. Too bad for Grace that she didn't close the latch on the case all the way, or her daughter might never have known she'd discovered it once again.

Dawn didn't confront her mother, but she finally did stop writing in her diary. She often wondered what Grace had thought about that. Neither of them had ever broached the subject, and they'd never discussed it. Dawn still didn't know what her mother had been expecting, hoping, or maybe even afraid to find. She had been a good kid, and Grace knew that. Her mother's behavior had never made any sense.

Dawn hadn't planned to tell anyone about her mother's snooping. Not even Lisa. It had seemed like her mother's dirty little secret. And hers too.

But secrets were hard to keep from best friends, especially when you were twelve years old. Dawn and Lisa borrowed each other's clothes, passed notes back and forth in math class, and spent hours on the phone wondering why all the boys went crazy over Lori Ruskin. They decided it must have been her boobs (or "boobies" as they'd called them back then), and they commiserated over their own flat chests. Dawn called Lisa the day she got her period, and Lisa told Dawn when she let Alex Harwood kiss her at Debbie Sandler's roller skating party.

So, one day after Lisa had wished for the millionth time that her own mother could be more like Grace, Dawn finally blurted it out.

"You don't know her, Lisa," she had screamed, jumping off the porch swing the girls had been sharing outside her parents' front door. Turning to face her best friend, she clamped her hands to her hips, bending her arms into opposing triangles. "You think you do, but you don't." She spat the words out. "You don't have a clue."

"Dawn!" Lisa's head jerked back, and her eyes narrowed into a squint. "What are you talking about? I know your mother. Are you kidding me?" She tilted her head and wrinkled her nose. "I know her almost as well as I know my own."

"Yeah Lisa, you know my mother," Dawn shot back, her voice a sarcastic singsong. "You know her the way *everyone* knows her." She shook her head and jammed her tongue into the roof of her mouth in a loud click. "But what you don't know is that the 'Grace'," she said, lifting her fingers in air quotes, "who doesn't nag, doesn't give me a curfew, and lets me have friends over whenever I want is also a snoop and an eavesdropper who has absolutely no respect for my privacy."

Lisa's eyes, locked with Dawn's, grew wide. She opened her mouth, then closed it.

Dawn wrapped her arms across her chest and looked

down at her sneakered feet. "And *that* is the way I live," she said quietly.

Dawn didn't remember the rest of their conversation, only that she and Lisa had sat together on that swing for a long, long time. She told Lisa everything. She trusted her best friend the way she wished her own mother had trusted *her*.

And at some point, probably around the time Dawn was getting ready to go off to college, Grace eased up on her surveillance tactics. She'd had to.

Unless she planned to move into the dorm with her daughter.

But now, even after so many years, the question still remained. Why had Grace, who in every other way had been the kind of mother any child would have wanted, taken on a relentless, one-woman, years-long quest to dig into her daughter's life? What secrets had she been trying to discover?

Any time Dawn had asked her mother to explain, Grace would put her off with the same clichéd responses. *I worried about you. That was my job. When you become a mother, you'll understand.*

Well, Dawn had been a mother for more than fourteen years, and she still didn't understand. She couldn't. But what she *could* do was to forgive. And she had done that a long time ago.

With a soft yawn, she lifted the airplane armrest and nuzzled her head into her husband's shoulder.

27

Everything Grace needed for her week with Joanna had fit into two bags. She'd packed her clothing, toiletries, and a book in a single duffel. She didn't need much, and anyway, she'd be back at her own house every day to visit with Hendrix. A large tote held the scrapbook and supplies, along with Joanna's blue folder stuffed with headlines and photos.

The blue folder...Grace hadn't opened it since the night Joanna had shown it to her, the night she'd feigned illness. It had been a shock. Seeing Charlie's face...she hadn't been prepared. But it didn't mean anything, and it had nothing to do with her. Or with her family. She had been surprised. That's all. Just surprised.

She stashed the bags in her trunk and climbed into her car, dropping her cell phone onto the passenger seat. As she reached for the seat belt, the phone buzzed. Turning her head, she looked down at the lighted screen.

Paula.

What did she want now? Grace had sent her a check the day after they'd met in New York. That should have been the end of it, the last page of the one horrible chapter in the otherwise happy story of Grace's life. Actually, it wasn't even a chapter, not even a page or a paragraph, just a single sentence about an otherwise unremarkable night more than fifty years ago.

So, what did Paula want? The rekindling of a long dead relationship? The illusion of a friendship? What?

Grace let the call go to voicemail, snapped on her seat belt, and turned the key in the ignition. The car rumbled to life, and with her foot still pressing on the brake, she peered down at her cell phone. The tiny red circle indicating a new voice message mocked her, daring her to ignore it. Might as well get it over with. She scooped up the phone, tapped the icon, and listened to the familiar voice.

"Hi Gracie, it's me...Paula. I did get your...uh...envelope in the mail. Thanks. But I do need you to call me back. I have another favor to ask you. A small one this time. I promise." She giggled in that sickening, high-pitched way of hers. "So, call me back. Okay?"

Grace clicked the phone off and tossed it back onto the seat.

"So, call me back. Okay?" she said out loud, her voice a shrill impression of Paula's. "Yeah, I'll call you back," she muttered, "when I'm good and ready."

She backed down the driveway and switched on the radio. Bob Dylan's sandpaper voice sang out his wish for an unknown someone to remain "forever young." But Grace wasn't in the mood, not even for Dylan. She turned the radio off and drove in silence, her hands locked in a vise-like grip around the steering wheel.

≈

The chirping beep of a tripped alarm system greeted her the moment she stepped inside Dawn and Tom's house. Dropping her bags by the door, she raced to the keypad and punched in the code, holding her breath until the flashing red light turned solid green. Although their house had secure locks on all the doors––windows too––and was situated in a safe suburban neighborhood, Dawn and Tom had the alarm system installed as soon as they moved in. It seemed like all the young people around here did that. Grace didn't meddle in her daughter and son-in-law's decisions, but she held her ground every time they tried to talk her into installing an alarm system in her own house. They'd given up on that battle a long time ago.

She looked down at her watch. It was 2:30. Joanna wouldn't be home for another hour, so she had time to get herself settled in before her granddaughter arrived. Hanging her jacket in the closet, she slung her duffel bag over her shoulder and headed up the stairs. At the top, she turned left, her rubber-soled shoes squeaking on the hardwood floor.

The door to Dawn and Tom's room was open. It felt like an invitation. So different from the young Dawn's room that Grace remembered. Her daughter must have been around eleven or twelve when she started closing her door. She didn't put up a sign, but it had been a clear signal. *Keep out, Mom.*

Grace had ignored the unspoken message. She had to make sure. She had to...She had to *know*. So, like a detective on the trail of...something...anything, she had searched Dawn's room. Routinely. She sifted through her drawers and rummaged through her closet, carefully returning each of her things to its place. She read her diaries, and she eavesdropped on her conversations. She watched, and she listened. She hovered, ever vigilant, always on the lookout for warning signs, clues to potential trouble looming ahead. And she had found...

Nothing. Absolutely nothing. Just evidence of her daughter's typical adolescent preoccupation with friends, clothes, boys, and school.

Grace had kept her worries to herself. She never mentioned the nightmarish possibility that flitted across her mind on sleepless nights that her beautiful and beloved daughter could conceivably be the result of a single careless mistake she had made on a long-ago night in San Francisco. She never shared that worry with anyone. Ever. She had carried that secret, a heavy rock trapped within a dangerous tangle of thorny questions, alone.

As the years passed, Dawn grew into a happy, good-natured young woman who had many friends, but was never part of a clique and was certainly never the leader of a pack. Any pack. The weight of Grace's secret became lighter and lighter until one day soon after her daughter had left for college, she walked past her old room without even peering inside. At that moment, she realized that the crushing weight of the worry she'd kept hidden for years had disappeared. Poof! Just like that. She knew then, and she knew now, without a sliver of doubt or a speck of fear, that the one night in San Francisco that had haunted her for years was exactly that—no more and no less. It was a single night, a night that had happened, but a night that had left her, her husband, and her daughter untouched, unscathed, and lucky.

But now, Paula had bulldozed her way back into Grace's life, and based on the absurd, far-fetched fantasy she'd concocted in her mind, she was preying on her former friend. Paula had actually become a de facto blackmailer. Any idea she might have had that Dawn was the child of...

She was crazy.

Paula had had a hard life, that was true, but she'd brought much of it upon herself with her own reckless behavior and bad decision-making. Still, what she was doing now––to Grace––was wrong. It was immoral, and it was evil. And there would never be an end to it, not as long as Grace kept sending her money. Maybe she should have called Paula's bluff the day they'd met instead of agreeing to send her a check so quickly.

What was done was done, but Grace wasn't going to compound her mistake. She'd had some time to think about it, and...

What could Paula actually do? What *would* she do? Tell Dawn that she and Grace had gone to a party more than fifty years ago in the house where Charles Manson lived? That they *might* have had drug-induced sex with a random someone in that house? Who would that *someone* be? And how would Paula prove it? No, Grace would not let that happen. She had given Paula two thousand dollars as a gift to an old friend in need. But that would be it. Paula had overplayed her hand, and Grace was done. Finished. She pressed her lips together and shook her head as she realized what she would have to do.

She'd call Paula back, when *she* was ready, and wish her well. Then she would say good-bye, casting her former best friend and current blackmailer out of her life. Forever. Because deep in her heart, Grace knew, she truly *knew*, that none of Paula's wild fantasies had the remotest chance of being true.

She stood in the doorway of the master bedroom without stepping inside. The king-sized bed was covered with a pearl gray comforter, and both of the matching night tables were stacked with books and magazines. A portrait of Dawn and Tom holding baby Joanna rested on a low table next to another pile of books and a small flat screen television.

At the other end of the hall, the door to Joanna's room was open. Stopping in front of it, Grace peered inside. Moving her head in slow motion, her mouth stretched into a wide smile as she took in the poster-bedecked walls—an aerial shot of Golden Gate Park and blown-up photos of an impossibly young Crosby, Stills, Nash, and Young, a guitar-wielding Jimi Hendrix, and a boa-wearing Janis Joplin. A fluorescent image of a flaming orange peace sign set against a rainbow-colored background hung over the desk.

The posters transported Grace back in time. Her chest filled with a tingly warmth, and she wrapped her arms around herself. This was going to be a wonderful week.

She would deal with Paula when she was good and ready.

Assuming she would deal with her at all.

28

J oanna's bus lumbered to a stop in front of the Lindstroms' house. Julie and Caitlin made their way down the aisle, giggling and waving to their friends as usual. *Let's go*, Joanna wanted to yell. Finally, the girls stepped off the bus, swiveling their heads in unison and lifting their hands in a final wave. The door closed with a metallic groan, and the bus began to move.

Joanna peered out her window, impatiently gazing at the familiar parade of McMansions, each sporting a weed-free lawn and ornamental landscaping. At the stop sign, her body lurched as the bus made a sharp turn onto her street. Slinging her backpack over her shoulder, she slid to the edge of her seat.

Four more houses, and the bus stopped in front of her own. Finally.

Jumping out of her seat, Joanna hurried to the front of the bus and out the door. She dashed up the driveway past Grace-ma's blue Beetle and raced up the steps leading to her house. Just as she reached for the door handle, it swung open.

"Grace-ma!" she yelped, flinging herself into her grandmother's outstretched arms.

Grace-ma pulled Joanna into a hug, pressing her to her chest and kissing the top of her head. Joanna breathed in the sandalwood scent of her grandmother's skin and ran her hand down the silvery blonde braid hanging over her shoulder. Her hair was soft and smooth.

"My Joanna," Grace-ma whispered and slid her hands down Joanna's arms, giving her elbows a gentle squeeze. Stepping back into the foyer, she swept her arm out behind her. "Come in. Come in."

Joanna followed her inside, dropping her backpack by the door. "Smells good in here." She closed her eyes and sniffed the air. "Chocolate chip cookies, but something else too."

Grace-ma smiled, her arms across her chest. "Uh-huh." She nodded.

"It smells kind of green." Joanna sniffed again, loudly this time. "Herbal."

Grace-ma inhaled slowly. "Yeah, I guess it does," she said. "It's chamomile tea." She danced into the kitchen, crooking her finger to beckon Joanna. "And you know I couldn't come here without bringing cookies, right?" she called over her shoulder.

Grace-ma, resplendent in an embroidered peasant shirt, long Indian print skirt, and a stack of silver bracelets, looked like an enchanting visitor from another place and time who had been teleported into the polished wood and granite kitchen. She set a pair of gleaming white mugs on the table, and Joanna pulled the matching plates from the cabinet. They sat, and Grace-ma poured the tea.

Joanna reached for a cookie and bit into it. Her "mmm," came out in a long, drawn-out sigh. She closed her eyes and

chewed. The melted chocolate blended into a buttery soft-
ness that caressed her mouth. Swallowing, she looked at her
grandmother's beaming face.

"Your cookies are the absolute best!" she said. "Even
better than Mom's."

Grace-ma put a finger to her lips. "Don't tell her that,"
she said with a laugh.

Joanna leaned forward, her chest pressing into the table.
"We'll have a whole week of things not to tell her," she said
in an exaggerated whisper.

Grace-ma clapped her hands together, and her green
eyes twinkled like a pair of gleaming emeralds. "Oh, yes!"
she chirped, bobbing her head up and down.

A warm tingle crept up Joanna's body and down her
arms. She adored her Grace-ma and loved to make her
happy. There was a special and unique bond between them,
magical and rare. But in truth, Joanna had never told or
shown her anything she wouldn't have shared with her own
mother. There was a part of herself she needed to keep
hidden. Even from Grace-ma. She wouldn't understand. No
one would.

But that was normal. Everyone had secrets. Grace-ma
probably even had a few of her own.

"So..." Grace-ma smiled and dabbed at her mouth with a
napkin. "How was school today?"

How was school today?

An ordinary question, but Joanna didn't know how to
answer it.

Should she say that her classes were boring? That she
got A's without trying? That Ryan wanted her to be his "offi-
cial" girlfriend? Or should she confess the deeper truth?
That she spent her days at school, long stretches of time

from early morning until the dismissal bell rang at three, thinking about Quinn.

Obsessing about Quinn. Agonizing over Quinn. Hating Quinn.

Over and over and over, Joanna replayed in her mind the way Quinn held court at the lunch table, turning every conversation to New York City––the parties at NYU, her brother's hot friends, and the "cooler than you can imagine" bars that didn't check IDs. And then there was the way she dangled the unspoken invitation, "maybe the next time I go..." and how Paige, Erin, and Megan, open-mouthed and wide-eyed like a trio of fish fixated on a brightly colored lure, leaned toward her in hopeful anticipation. A white-hot anger burned in Joanna's chest every time she thought about it.

"School?" She looked at Grace-ma, her face a neutral mask, and shrugged. "Nothing new. Same old, same old."

"What about the fire? Mom told me about it. Did they ever find out who set it?"

"Nope." Joanna shook her head. "They think it started when someone dropped a cigarette in the garbage can in the girls' room." She tapped her foot on the floor, a soft drumbeat. "That's what I heard anyway."

"So, they think it was accidental?"

Joanna pushed her lips together and opened her mouth with a loud smack. "I guess," she said, raising her eyebrows.

Grace-ma crossed her arms in her lap, cupping her elbows. "And what do *you* think?" she asked.

Joanna gripped her mug, letting its warmth creep into her fingers. Then, with three words and a slow, deliberate shake of her head, she answered her grandmother's question the only way she could.

"I don't know," she said, pushing the lie out of her

mouth. She planted her elbows on the table and lowered her chin onto her folded hands. "I really don't."

"Do you think it's Quinn?" Grace-ma whispered.

Joanna waited, letting the name hang in the air. She opened her mouth and then closed it. Breathing in and then out, she lifted her shoulders in a big, slow shrug.

"Joanna, listen to me," Grace-ma said, her voice an uncharacteristic command. "Stay away from her."

"I really don't have much to do with her."

Grace-ma nodded and glanced up at the ceiling. Her jaw tightened, and the pair of shallow lines bracketing her mouth deepened into a twin parenthesis of wrinkles. Her chest moved up and down as she exhaled a drawn-out sigh and turned back to her granddaughter.

"Lie down with pigs, Joanna, and you'll get dirty," she said quietly. "Remember that."

Joanna cocked her head, and her mouth twisted into a smirk. "Is that the same as 'if you lie down with dogs, you'll wake up with fleas'?"

"I'm serious, Joanna. Stay away from her. Please."

Joanna reached across the table, caught hold of her grandmother's hand, and squeezed it gently. "I'm not involved with her, Grace-ma. Really. You don't have to worry."

"I know, but sometimes if you associate with..." Grace-ma's voice trailed off, and she shook her head. "Never mind. You're a smart girl with nice friends." She lifted Joanna's hand to her mouth and kissed it. "I'm not worried."

Joanna wanted to believe those words, but her grandmother's narrowed eyes and wrinkled brow told her the truth.

Soon enough though, and Grace-ma's worries, as well as her own, would be over.

29

"Stop thanking me, Dawn," Grace said into the phone. "A week with Joanna? You know what a treat this is for me."

"But now you have to go to Back-to-School Night too. You'll have to drive by yourself, and you won't be home until late. But wait...I could ask someone to take you. I'm sure––"

"Dawn, stop," Grace said. "I can drive. I can drive by myself. Even at night." She laughed. "I'm not *that* old."

"Mom, I didn't mean that. It's just––"

"Never mind 'it's just'. I can do it, Dawn. I *want* to do it. I haven't gone to a Back-to-School Night since *you* were in high school."

"Maybe it's just that I wish I could go," Dawn said, her voice lowering to a whisper. "If Tom hadn't already bought the plane tickets, I never would have––"

"Dawn, please. This is your vacation with your husband. Just the two of you. You've always been there for Joanna, and she knows that. There'll be other Back-to-School Nights."

Dawn's long sigh whooshed through the phone.

"How about if I take notes and report back to you? Would that make you feel better?"

"I guess," Dawn said softly.

"Good. Now say good-bye, and enjoy your time with Tom."

"Good-bye, Mom," Dawn said. "But remember to take notes."

"Don't worry. I will. Good-bye, Dawn." Grace laughed and clicked off the phone.

Still smiling, she opened the dishwasher and began to unload it, carefully stacking plates and lining glasses along the edge of the counter. She'd already been back to her own house to feed Hendrix and to give him a long massage, moving her hands from his back to his belly to the front of his ears and ending at the sweet spot under his chin. They both knew the routine, and it was just as relaxing for Grace as it was for Hendrix. In fact, sleeping with him curled up against the backs of her legs was the only thing she missed since she'd been staying with Joanna. Other than that, her week with her granddaughter was a perfect staycation with her best buddy.

Each morning, after a gulp of orange juice, Joanna would scarf down a bowl of oatmeal, quickly peck her grandmother's cheek, and dash down the driveway just in time to catch the school bus. That left Grace with plenty of time for a power walk through the neighborhood, a trip back to her own house to feed and tend to Hendrix, a quick shower, and a stop at the grocery store before heading back to her daughter's.

She reserved the half hour before Joanna got home from school for some reading time in Dawn's favorite sun-warmed chair under the wide bay window in their book-lined living room. When she heard the rumble of the bus coming down the street, she'd hurry to the door, opening it in time to see Joanna rushing up the driveway, her long dark hair streaming out behind her. Grace would then pull her into a warm, tight hug, and they'd settle down for a snack.

As they bit into cookies and sipped tea, Grace would listen to a detailed recounting of Joanna's day, a whirlwind narrative leapfrogging from her mastery of the one-armed plank in gym class to her annoyance with Ryan's relentless attention. With an elbow on the table and a hand pressed to her cheek, Grace would gaze at her beautiful granddaughter and smile.

Joanna let her inside in a way Dawn never did, but Grace knew that had been her own fault. This time she was doing it right, and her relationship with Joanna was simple, uncomplicated, and honest.

While Grace prepared dinner, Joanna would head upstairs to do her homework. Later, after they had eaten and cleaned the kitchen together, they'd watch *Jeopardy!* (Joanna was much better than Grace, even beating out most of the contestants on TV) and *Law & Order* reruns.

Grace glanced at the digital clock on the microwave. Joanna wouldn't be home for another two hours. Plenty of time to do a load of wash. She headed up the stairs, grabbed her denim laundry bag from the bottom of the guest room closet, and made her way to Joanna's room. Inhaling a mix of sandalwood and vanilla, her eyes darted to the dresser, home to a colorful assortment of well-used candles and a collection of incense sticks set into tiny ceramic holders.

She dropped her laundry bag by the door and walked into the center of the room. Tilting her head back, she pivoted slowly. Walls papered with posters of sixties rock icons with wild hair and blazing eyes, closet doors festooned with tie-dyed scarves, mirrors and lampshades draped with beaded necklaces, and a queen-sized bed adorned with an Indian print bedspread––the room spoke of Joanna. It spoke of Grace too.

Once, many years ago, she had lived in a room like this. After she had returned from San Francisco––before she'd known she was pregnant, before she'd married Doug––she had transformed her teenage bedroom, replacing her flowered comforter with a swirling paisley-pattered spread and swapping her ballerina jewelry box and silver comb and brush set for a trio of woven baskets and a lava lamp. Her walls had sported concert posters and blown-up photos of sunsets and rainbows. Now here, in her granddaughter's room, Grace's only reminder that fifty years had passed was the flat screen TV perched on the edge of the dresser and the thin silver laptop resting on the desk.

Over the last year or so, Joanna had launched an aggressive campaign aimed at convincing Grace, in her words, to "expand your world, Grace-ma." Of course, to a fourteen-year-old, the best way of doing that was by jumping head-first into cyberspace. Two nights earlier, seated next to Grace with her laptop open on the table in front of them, Joanna had insisted on leading her grandmother through a personalized tour of "the whole world that's out there."

"Just think about it, Grace-ma, you can do your shopping online without leaving your house. You can look up recipes. Books too. You can even read excerpts on the computer. And you can find the answer to anything you want to know, like for example––"

"Okay, okay. I give up," Grace had said, holding her hands up and laughing. "But just so you know, it's not like I'm a total computer illiterate. I do email sometimes, and I did sign up for Medicare online—although someone at the library did help me with that." She smirked.

Joanna nodded. "I know, Grace-ma, but there's so much more you could be doing."

So, for the next hour Grace had allowed her granddaughter to guide her in and out of a maze of websites, blogs, and online stores. And Joanna was right. There was indeed "a whole world out there."

Crossing the room, Grace settled into the desk chair and ran her hand over the smooth lid of her granddaughter's laptop. How about some early Christmas shopping? According to Joanna, Amazon.com was the site that had everything. She flipped the laptop open and touched her finger to the trackpad. But the blue-gray screen and invitation to log in as "Guest" that Joanna had shown her wasn't there.

Instead, she was greeted with a Google search bar displaying the words "car fires" and a checkerboard of fiery images of twisted metal followed by a list of websites ranging from news reports to how-to instructions to most likely causes.

She snapped the lid of the laptop closed and slid her chair back from the desk. Her heartbeat quickened into a rapid staccato pounding inside her chest, and her legs went tingly and numb.

Why had Joanna been researching car fires?

An icy coldness invaded her body, and she shivered, wrapping her arms across her chest. Her mouth went dry. An onslaught of questions pummeled her brain.

Had Joanna been trying to figure out if Quinn really had set the school bathroom fire? Was she planning to tell her friends the truth about Quinn's past? Was she trying to protect her own family's car from something Quinn *might* do? Or maybe, hopefully, was this nothing more than normal teenage curiosity about "the new girl?"

Still, it didn't make sense. Why would Joanna...?

Grace shook her head, shooing the questions away, and opened the closet door. Snatching up Joanna's laundry bag and grabbing her own, she headed down the stairs.

30

Today would be different. Joanna would be different. Or more accurately, she would *act* differently. Because today was the day she would put her plan into effect. And Joanna had always been good at both of those things—planning and acting.

The bus rolled to a stop at the foot of the long driveway leading to Quinn's house, her "huge and absolutely beautiful" house according to Paige. From her seat, Joanna could see only the thick grove of trees hiding the house from view.

Decked out in her usual beret and sunglasses, Quinn climbed onto the bus and strode down the aisle, the thump-thump of her boots adding a thudding bass line to the chorus of everyday school bus chatter.

Joanna stretched her mouth into a happy-to-see-you smile. "Hey, Quinn," she chirped as the other girl tossed her backpack onto the seat in front of hers.

Quinn froze, her feet rooted to the floor. Her mouth opened, closed, then opened again. "Hi, Joanna," she said, cocking her head to the side. The corners of her lips turned up in a fake-looking smile, and she slid into her seat, her back to Joanna.

Joanna leaned forward and reached her hand out. Should she tap Quinn's shoulder? Make conversation? Nah...too much all-of-a-sudden friendliness. She pulled her hand back and dropped it into her lap. Best not to overdo it.

Mr. Reed spent the whole of first period going over geometry proofs. Joanna focused on the back of Quinn's head, her beret a black circle against the whiteness of her hair. Quinn reached down to scratch her leg and then leaned back in her chair. She's probably just as bored as I am, Joanna thought.

When the bell finally rang, Quinn snatched up her books and headed out of the classroom. Paige walked out with Joanna and then with a quick "see ya at lunch," raced to catch up with Quinn.

Joanna nodded and kept walking. Smiling at Quinn was one thing, but running after her? *That* was not going to happen.

In history class, Mrs. Bergstrom didn't give Joanna the chance to further her new Quinn-friendly strategy either. First, it was a fill-in-the-blank quiz on the Louisiana Purchase:

It _doubled_ the size of the United States.

The president at the time was _Thomas Jefferson_.

Etcetera. Etcetera. Etcetera.

Next came a lecture on the causes of the War of 1812. Blah, blah, blah. Mrs. B. droned on for twenty minutes straight before looking up at the clock.

"Well, it looks like that's it for today," she said with a curt bow of her head. "For homework, please read––"

The end-of-period bell rang, interrupting her, and the room erupted with sound. Chairs were pushed back, books were shoved into backpacks, and the low-pitched buzz of whispered conversations grew into a loud free-for-all.

Mrs. B. lifted her hand in a stop-and-listen sign. "Students, please," she called out over the din. "Read chapter five for tomorrow."

Quinn, already at the door, glanced back at Mrs. B. Joanna, in her line of sight, smiled and waved. With a blank expression plastered on her face, Quinn looked directly at Joanna and lowered her head in a single nod. Her mouth curled up into a perfunctory close-lipped smile, and with a quick pivot, she turned back to the door and strutted out of the classroom.

Joanna walked out with Erin and Megan, both of them complaining about the length of the chapter they had been assigned to read that night, both of them oblivious to Joanna's little dance with Quinn.

This might be even easier than Joanna had thought. And she only had one more class before lunch. Yoga. No pressure there. Just peace and tranquility.

But anchored on her blue mat, Joanna found herself struggling. She maneuvered her body into the sequence of positions she'd been taught, but her limbs were wooden, and her breathing was off. Too shallow, too fast. The poses that had always come so easily felt artificial and forced. Joanna relied on muscle memory to perform the familiar routine while her mind traveled, mapping out her next moves.

Her thinking mimicked that of a master chess player. And to her great advantage, her opponent wasn't even aware of the game, and more importantly, that she was in it. Joanna was the one with the plan, and she knew exactly what she needed to do—step by step by step. By the following week she would be back to yoga breathing and mindfulness.

The class wound down with the Child's Pose. The students, chests resting on their thighs, brought their heads to the floor and stretched their arms out onto their mats. From there, they moved into the Corpse position. Joanna rolled onto her back, and with her legs apart and her arms resting at her sides, she forced her eyes to close.

"Namaste," Ms. Burke said in her oh-so-zen voice, and the class was over.

Jerking her body upright, Joanna jumped off the mat and darted into the locker room. In a flash, she was stripping off her leggings and tank top and changing back into her jeans and peasant shirt. She'd already stuffed all the books she would need for the next two periods into her backpack, so she didn't have to stop at her locker before lunch.

Ready, set, go.

With her head down and her elbows out, Joanna sped down the crowded hallways and made her way to the bank of vending machines outside the cafeteria's double doors. She pulled a sheaf of dollar bills from her wallet, and one by one, fed them into the beverage machine. One, two, three, four, five bottles of water. She slipped them into her backpack and hurried into the cafeteria.

The room was a sea of evenly spaced rows of rectangular tables, a few dotted with books and backpacks, most of them still empty. Joanna was early. That was a first. She marched over to her group's usual table, slid into a seat, and dropped her backpack onto the floor. Bending to reach inside, she plunged her hand past the bottles and pulled out four books. One by one, she positioned them in front of each of the four seats surrounding her own. Table secured. Leaning back in her chair, she stretched her legs out under the table and settled in to wait. It didn't take long.

Megan was the first to arrive. She moved quickly for a chubby girl, but her open-mouthed pant and flushed face revealed the effort of her rush to save their regular table. Joanna knew that Megan tried to please her, in ways both large and small, and basked in the sunshine of her approval. She was a true "friend." Kind of like a loyal dog.

"You're here early." Megan tossed her books onto the table and claimed the seat next to Joanna.

"I guess." Joanna shrugged.

Megan scraped her chair back and jumped up. "I'll get us a place on line."

"No, that's okay. I'll go up with you," Joanna said, touching Megan's fleshy arm. "Let's just wait a few minutes for the others."

"Really?" Megan's eyebrows shot up. "You sure? You don't want me to—?"

"No, we can all go up together," Joanna said. "Might as well."

"Uh...okay...sure, we can wait." Megan plopped back into her chair.

Her forehead crinkled, and her face twisted into a mask of bewilderment. Of course, she was confused. Why wouldn't she be? Ever since the girls were all in middle school, she, along with Erin and Paige, had been getting to the cafeteria ahead of Joanna. They'd drop their books on the table and snag a spot on the food line, making sure to grab a tray for Joanna. Then, a strategic five minutes later, Joanna would come sauntering in and step right into the place they'd saved for her. She might have gotten a dirty look from someone here and there, but who cared? That had been their routine for the last couple of years.

But all of a sudden, Joanna was giving up her privileged position in their—no, *her*—little group? Guess it did *look* that way. Joanna kept her face neutral, fighting off the smile that threatened to curve her lips.

The room began to fill as students drifted inside. Erin, trailed by Paige, and then Quinn, headed over to the table, their eyes all on Joanna. Erin pulled her bottom lip into her mouth, Paige tilted her head and narrowed her eyes, and Quinn smirked.

Paige dropped her books and placed her hands, fingers splayed, on the table and leaned toward Joanna. "What are *you* doing here?" she asked.

Joanna didn't like Paige's tone. She didn't like the way the girl thrust her chin out when she called Joanna "you." She didn't like the way she leaned just a bit too close, invading Joanna's space. She didn't like...a lot of things. But Joanna kept her body still, refusing to back away. Paige had always been difficult—a little too aggressive, a little too questioning, a little too unappreciative. And since Quinn's arrival, she was becoming impossible.

But that was going to change, and it was going to change soon.

"I didn't have to stop at my locker." Joanna shrugged. "I even had time to..." With her eyes still on Paige, she reached into her backpack and pulled out two bottles of water. She placed them on the table, grabbed the other three, and slid one in front of each of the girls. Paige, Megan, Erin, and Quinn. Then, with a Cheshire cat smile, she twisted the cap on her own bottle and brought it to her mouth.

Erin was the first to speak. "Wow, thanks!"

Then Megan. "That's so nice of you, Joanna. Thank you."

"Th-thanks?" Paige said, turning the word into a question.

Quinn rubbed the back of her neck and looked at Joanna. "Thank you," she said slowly.

"No problem," Joanna said and stood up. "Now, let's get some food."

She marched over to the cafeteria line without glancing back. She didn't have to. She knew they'd be following her. Little ducks in a row. Even Quinn. Reaching the stack of gray plastic trays, Joanna gathered up five of them, casually turning her head as she handed four to Megan to pass back. Yup, the girls were all there. Megan, Erin, Paige, and Quinn.

Pushing their trays along the metal track, they each opted for their standard choices. A burger and fries for Megan, a fajita for Erin, a chef salad for Paige, a turkey sandwich for Quinn., and minestrone soup and a vegetable wrap for Joanna.

Back at the table, the girls moved their books aside and settled in to eat. And to talk. The conversation started off with the usual chatter about the usual things. They dissected rumors about who had the hots for whom, complained about their teachers, griped about their parents, and argued about what would be the best new show coming to Netflix.

Quinn nodded along and moved her gaze from Paige to Erin to Megan to Joanna. It was Tuesday, and she had already told them about her "awesome" weekend in the city, and it was still too early to talk about (and maybe even include them in) her plans for the weekend. The cool people didn't plan that far in advance. Anyway, that was probably what Quinn thought.

Erin finished her whining rant about how her mother

wouldn't let her quit piano lessons and finally bit into her fajita.

Joanna seized her chance.

"So, I was thinking..." she began. Then pausing, she looked down at her wrap. Lifting it to her mouth, she bit into it, and started to chew. Slowly.

Four pairs of eyes zeroed in on her face. She swallowed, patted her lips with a napkin, and reached for her water.

"Yeah...?" Erin said, leaning forward.

"Well, you know my parents are away," Joanna said, letting her words hang in the air.

Paige's fork stopped midway to her mouth, and the speedy urgency of Megan's chewing slowed. Erin leaned across the table, bringing her face close enough for Joanna to smell the sharp tang of fajita on her breath. Quinn bit into her sandwich.

"Grace-ma's staying with me, but she said I could have people over Friday night if I want to," Joanna said matter-of-factly and leaned back in her chair.

"People?" said Paige.

"Yeah," Joanna said. "Like you guys." She tossed her hand out in a wide wave, careful to include all of her girls. *And* Quinn. "And Ryan and some of his friends," she said, jerking her head back toward his table. "Brett, Matt, Dan." She ticked the names off on her fingers. "Maybe some of the others. We'll see."

"That sounds good." Paige's head bobbed in a quick nod.

"I'm in," Erin said.

Megan swallowed her food. "Me too."

Joanna turned toward Quinn.

"I can be there," she said coolly.

As if that mattered...

Joanna hadn't actually asked her grandmother yet, but

that wouldn't be a problem. And she was sure Ryan and his crew would be happy to hang at her house.

"Okay then. It's a plan." She tightened her lips around her smile and reached for what was left of her wrap.

Yeah, it was a plan alright.

If you can't beat 'em, join 'em. Joanna was sure that's what they all thought her change in attitude toward Quinn was about.

If they only knew…

But they didn't. And they wouldn't.

Not even when Quinn couldn't make it to her little house party Friday night.

31

Grace slowed down as she drove past the line of yellow buses parked along the narrow roadway in front of the high school. She turned into the side lot, where Joanna had told her to wait, and slid into a parking space. The gray metal door facing the lot swung open and closed, repeatedly following some sort of mysterious rhythm. Students—alone, in pairs, and in packs—spilled out into the late afternoon sunshine.

Watching for Joanna, she kept her eyes on the door. Her hands were cold, and the back of her neck prickled. Nerves? So strange for her to feel that way right before she saw her granddaughter. But Grace needed to know why she'd been researching car fires. She hadn't been ready to bring it up when Joanna came home from school the previous day or even later that evening. She hadn't known what to say. But somehow, she needed to answer the question that had been buzzing through her brain like a relentless mosquito.

Why?

She couldn't let Joanna think she'd been snooping around in her room. Grace was sure Dawn had told her stories about *that*. But she did need to know what was going on. And why.

The metal door burst open, and Joanna sprang out. Shading her eyes with her hand, she slowly turned her head and scanned the sea of cars, looking for the Volkswagen Beetle. Grace stepped out and lifted her arm in a gentle wave. Joanna's mouth widened into a smile, and she raced toward her grandmother. She moved like a deer, graceful and quick. Grace's lungs filled with air, and her chest swelled.

"Grace-ma!" Joanna yelped, diving in for a hug.

Grace pulled her close, burying her face in her granddaughter's shiny dark hair. She smelled of lemons. Fresh and clean. Young. Innocent.

Joanna gave her grandmother a tight squeeze, then stepped back. "It's so nice of you to pick me up today." She tilted her head, raising her eyebrows. "So...?"

"So?" Grace laughed.

"So, what's the occasion?"

"Does there have to be an occasion for me to pick my granddaughter up from school?" Grace asked, not waiting for an answer. "Get in," she said and slid into the driver's seat.

"Okay," Joanna said with a grin and walked around the car to open the passenger side door. Dropping her backpack on the floor, she settled into the seat and buckled her seatbelt. "So, now you have to tell me. Where are we going?"

"Well, since we only have four more nights together before your parents come home..."

Joanna pushed her lower lip out in an exaggerated pout.

"And since fall's here, and pretty soon it'll be cold, I thought we'd head over to *Thompson's* for ice cream." Grace leaned over to pat her granddaughter's arm. "It's even warm enough for us to sit outside."

"Ooh...let's go!" Joanna drummed her hands against her thighs.

Grace put the car into drive and headed out of the parking lot. But her mind wasn't on driving, and it wasn't on ice cream either. She needed to figure out why Joanna had developed a sudden interest in car fires. Somehow, she had to bring the conversation around to Quinn, and she needed to do it while she was still driving, her eyes on the road. It had to be just a casual chat. Nothing more. Her heartbeat quickened like a hummingbird in flight. She breathed in and then out, slow and deep, forcing her body, if not her mind, to relax.

And then Joanna spoke.

"Oh, I need to tell you something, Grace-ma," she said. "Remember how I was upset about Quinn? How I thought she was trying to take over my group of friends?"

"Yes, of course, I remember," Grace said evenly, her hands tightening on the wheel.

"Well, I don't have to worry about that anymore."

Grace shot Joanna a sidelong glance. "No?"

"Nope." The word burst out of her mouth with a popping sound. She clamped her lips together and shook her head from side to side.

"What happened?" Grace stole another glance at her granddaughter.

Joanna leaned back into her seat. "She moved to another lunch table."

"What?" Grace's eyebrows lowered, and her eyes narrowed into a squint. "Why did she do that?"

"I don't know. It happened today. She got to lunch after

the rest of us. Then she walked over to another table and sat down."

"Who was at the other table? Do you know them?"

"Not really. I just know they're the kids who smoke behind the school every morning."

"What did your friends say about her sitting there?" Grace asked, keeping her eyes on the road.

"Well, you know Paige." Joanna sighed dramatically. "She said Quinn knew those kids from one of her classes. I guess she wanted the rest of us to think that she and Quinn were still BFFs."

"What about Erin and Megan?"

Joanna shrugged. "I don't think they cared."

"And you?"

"I couldn't be happier," Joanna said. "I just hope she stays there."

"Me too." Grace nodded.

"Yeah, I don't want to have anything to do with that arsonist."

That arsonist.

And just like that, Joanna had given Grace an opening. But still, she needed to be careful. Very careful.

"Do you think she was the one who set the fire in the school bathroom?" Grace asked, careful to keep her tone light.

"I don't know. Maybe? Probably? But it's the car fire that really bothers me." She pushed her lips together and opened them with a loud smack. "In fact, I've been doing some research into it."

The car was at the intersection of Main and Broad, and the light had just turned yellow. Grace could have made it, but instead, she pressed down on the brake and turned toward Joanna. "You researched the fire she set to the teacher's car?"

"No." Joanna shook her head. "I've been reading about car fires in general on the internet," she said. "And looking at pictures," she added quietly.

"Why?" Grace's voice came out in a high-pitched squeak.

"I was thinking about telling Paige. Maybe Erin and Megan too." Joanna ran her tongue across her lips and swallowed. "But even if I don't, I wanted to know what kind of girl...uh...invaded––yeah, that's the word––*invaded*––our group."

"Hmm...I can understand that...why you might be concerned. But I am glad, *very* glad actually, that she seems to have moved on."

"So am I, Grace-ma," Joanna said. "So am I."

The light turned green, and the car behind them honked. Grace drove through the intersection, her hands light on the wheel.

Joanna switched off the lamp on her night table and sank back into her pillow. She'd sleep well tonight. Her 't's were crossed, her 'i's were dotted, and her ducks were lined up in a row. All clichés describing a careful and well-thought-out plan. All true. Acting out and convincing her girls of her intention to reach out to and include Quinn had been easy. A little distasteful maybe, but easy. It would be helpful though.

After Quinn was out of the picture, Joanna would have a firmer grip on her position as the group's unchallenged leader. Her gracious and open-hearted attitude toward the unfortunate Quinn would only strengthen her hold on the others.

Joanna, the magnanimous leader. *Ha!*

As for Grace-ma, that had been a bit more difficult. But with some delicate verbal maneuvering, she was able to handle that too, not that she should have had to.

Leaving her computer open to her last Google search had been a big mistake. Joanna wasn't usually careless like that, but she'd had a lot on her mind the past few days. When she got home from school yesterday, she'd found her laundry folded and piled on her bed—*so nice of Grace-ma*—but something had seemed just a bit off, a little out of place. Then she noticed that her laptop was not positioned in its usual spot on her desk. When she opened it...*oh jeez*...her car fire search! It wasn't Grace-ma's fault. Joanna had given her a computer mini-lesson the night before, and she had told her to feel free to use her laptop...

Joanna saw that Grace-ma was nervous when she picked her up after school. Her breathing was too deliberate, too controlled, and her hands were locked into that ten and two position on the steering wheel that no one used after they passed the driving test. But Joanna had been prepared.

She was the one to bring up Quinn, telling Grace-ma that the arsonist (key word "arsonist") had moved to another lunch table. That was the bait, and her grandmother had taken it, asking her if she thought Quinn had set the fire at school. From there, it was logical for Joanna to oh-so-inno-cently talk about her research into car fires. She had watched her grandmother's body relax as she spoke. It was in the set of her shoulders, the grip of her hands, and the rhythm of her breathing. Joanna's explanation was logical, and Grace-ma was happy to believe it.

She didn't want to lie, not to her grandmother, but it had been the right thing to do. For both of them.

Fifteen minutes later, as they licked their ice cream cones, Joanna had asked if she could have some friends over Friday night.

"Of course!" came her grandmother's predictable answer.

Closing her eyes and opening her mouth in a wide yawn, Joanna rolled over onto her side. Tomorrow was going to be a big day.

And night.

32

Back in her own house, just as Grace stepped into the den, Hendrix darted ahead of her and raced into the room, stopping at the foot of the over-stuffed chair positioned under the window. Shaking her head and smiling, Grace made her way to *their* favorite chair and sunk into it, laying her cordless phone on its arm.

"Okay, Hendrix, come on," she said, patting her lap. "I'm ready."

The cat looked up at her, and with a soft meow, jumped into her lap. He moved in a slow circle, kneading her thighs with his paws, staking his claim on her, before he curled up into a furry ball. After a few light strokes down his back, Grace moved her hand under his neck and rubbed, her touch a tender massage. He closed his eyes and began to purr like a gently humming motor.

Grace was having a wonderful week staying with Joanna while Dawn and Tom were away. Time with her grand-daughter was always a gift. But she did miss her own home and the many little touches––tinkling wind chimes, macramé plant hangers, and colorfully painted pottery––

that made it uniquely hers. Even more than that, she missed Hendrix, his quiet presence all day long and the soft warmth of him in her bed at night. She petted his head, and his eyes opened to half-mast for a moment before he drifted back to feline dreamland. It was the best way to relax––for both of them.

Only one thing marred the perfect peace of the moment, and that was Paula's voice message. Grace had tried to push it out of her thoughts by practicing mindfulness and concentrating on her breathing. But like the buzzing of a tiny gnat, it refused to go away.

She needed to deal with it, and she would.

After Dawn and Tom return, when she'd be spending the nights back in her own house, she'd call Paula, and she would end it. In just a few days, once and for all, Grace would say what she should have told her former friend in person.

Good-bye, Paula. Have a nice life.

Although that message would have to wait for another time, there was a phone call Grace did need to make just then, a call she actually wanted to make. She looked down at her wrist, nestled against her sleeping cat, and checked her watch. It was a few minutes past noon, which would make it 9 A.M. in California. It should be a good time to catch Dawn.

Grace had wanted to call the previous night. She'd been excited to share the good news about Quinn, eager to put her daughter's mind at rest, but she didn't want to risk Joanna overhearing her side of the conversation. Careful not to disturb Hendrix, she reached for her phone and dialed Dawn's number.

"Hi, Mom," she answered, her voice bright and chirpy.

"Good morning, Dawn. You sound happy."

Grace heard a muffled "Tom" followed by a giggle.

"I am," her daughter whispered into the phone.

"Good," Grace said, hearing the smile in her own voice. "Listen, I don't want to disturb you. You can call me back later if you want."

"No, no. It's fine, Mom. Tom's just going into the shower."

"Are you sure? Because I don't want to—"

"Mom, you're not interrupting anything. I want to talk to you. How's everything going? How's Joanna? And how are *you*?" she asked, her questions pouring out in a nonstop stream.

"Everything's good here. I'm really enjoying my time with Joanna, and I think she is too. I hope so, anyway."

"Oh, she definitely is. She told me how much she likes being with you," Dawn said. "I don't know how happy she'll be when Tom and I come back..." Her voice trailed off.

"Oh, Dawn, don't be silly. Of course, she'll be happy."

"Hmm...well...anyway, don't forget tonight is Back-to-School Night. It starts at seven, but you should get there at least fifteen minutes early. Okay?" She didn't wait for her mother's answer. "Because it'll be crowded. Just about all the freshman parents will be there, and you don't know your way around the school. I mean there are signs, but—"

"Dawn, Dawn..." Grace laughed. "Everything is under control. Joanna gave me detailed instructions, and I know exactly what to do."

"And don't forget to take notes, Mom. I want to know everything. Even if you don't think it's important, I want to—"

"I'll take notes, Dawn. Don't worry. I even have a notebook prepared," Grace said. "But I do have something else to tell you. Good news, in fact."

"Yeah? What?"

"Well, the good news is that..." Grace cleared her throat, enjoying the moment. "Joanna seems to think Quinn might be losing interest in her group of friends."

"Really? Why?"

"She told me that Quinn sat at another lunch table yesterday with some other kids, the ones who smoke. Maybe Joanna and her crew are too tame for her. Anyway, Joanna thinks Quinn might have found herself some new friends."

"That's great!" Dawn said. "But how does Joanna feel about it? Did she say?"

"Oh yes, she sure did." Grace snickered. "She said she didn't want to have anything to do with that arsonist. And those were her exact words––'that arsonist'."

"That *is* good news, Mom." Dawn's long exhale, loud enough for Grace to hear through the phone, was suddenly cut off with a quick gasp. "But wait, what about the others? Paige, Erin, and Megan. Especially Paige. How do they feel?"

"I asked Joanna that same question," Grace said. "She didn't think Erin and Megan cared, and Paige made sure to tell them all that Quinn already knew the kids at the other table from one of her classes." She clicked her tongue. "Guess it was a matter of pride to Paige. Anyway, the important thing is that our girl is happy."

"And that Quinn is out of the picture."

"Yes, that too. Definitely."

"Oh, Mom, just hold on a minute."

Grace could hear Tom's voice, soft but deep, and Dawn's whispered response. She couldn't make out their words. She didn't have to.

"Mom..."

"I know. Go ahead, honey. We'll talk later."

Dawn blew a kiss into the phone. "And thanks for telling me about Quinn, Mom. I love you."

"And I love you," Grace said. "Very much."

"Remember to take notes. Okay?"

"Yes, I'll remember. Just go back to your husband and enjoy your vacation."

"I will," she said. "And thank you, Mom."

"No thanks necessary. Now, say 'good-bye'." Grace's voice was a gentle command.

"Good-bye, Mom," came Dawn's giggly reply.

Grace returned the phone to the arm of her chair and leaned back. Dawn was happy, and without the disruption caused by Quinn, Joanna was happy too. So, instead of researching car fires, she could go back to…Well, she could go back to whatever it was that fourteen-year-old girls did these days.

All was right with the ones Grace loved. And very soon, after she called Paula, all would be right with her too. With her hands around Hendrix, anchoring him in her lap, she slid her hips forward and closed her eyes.

Ahh…Her body relaxed, and her breathing slowed.

33

"I'll finish the dishes, Grace-ma. You should get going." Joanna touched her grandmother's shoulder, nudging her away from the sink.

"I'm almost done. Just want to wash this last pot," Grace-ma said, her voice almost drowned out by the sound of running water.

"You're gonna get in trouble." Joanna laughed. "Mom said—"

"I know what your mother said, Joanna. 'Get there fifteen minutes early', and I'm going to do just that. Don't you worry." Grace-ma turned the water off and set the pot upside down on the drying rack.

Snatching up a towel, Joanna flicked it at her grandmother and reached for the pot.

"Okay, okay. I'm going," Grace-ma said with an exaggerated sigh and a smile. "I just need a couple of minutes, and I'll be ready."

Joanna listened to the sound of her grandmother's footsteps, deliberate and slow, as she climbed the stairs. Tapping the edge of the counter, she looked down at her watch.

Grace-ma needed to get going. Her heart beat in a shallow, fluttery rhythm, and she inhaled, counting...*One, two, three.* She opened her mouth and breathed out. Sliding the dried pot into the cabinet under the stove, she draped the towel over the rack.

Grace-ma came back into the kitchen, wearing jeans and low-heeled boots topped with a knitted poncho and an embroidered scarf.

Joanna stepped into her hug. "You look more like a student than a grandmother," she said, tugging on the scarf.

Grace-ma stepped back and chuckled. "Did I ever tell you that you're my favorite grandchild?"

"I'm your *only* grandchild, Grace-ma," Joanna said, rolling her eyes.

"But you're still my favorite. Now, off I go to see what exactly it is that you do in school all day long."

"Don't believe any of it." Joanna laughed. "Just drive safely, okay?"

"Yes, ma'am." Grace-ma lifted her hand in a mock salute.

Joanna followed her to the door, and after locking it behind her, headed into the dining room. Peering through the slatted blinds, she watched as her grandmother climbed into her Volkswagen Beetle. The headlights flicked on, and the car moved down the driveway. It came to a full stop and then made a right turn onto the street.

Now, it was time for *her* to get ready.

Back-to-School Night. Just about all the freshmen parents would be at the high school following abbreviated versions of their kids' schedules and meeting their teachers. Joanna and her classmates would be at home. Or that's where they were *supposed* to be.

She raced up the stairs and into her room. Moving quickly, she slipped into a pair of black leggings and pulled on a matching hooded sweatshirt. She grabbed her back-pack and ran down to the main level where she gathered up a box of kitchen matches, a few sheets of newspaper, and an empty detergent bottle plucked from the recycling bucket. Snatching the key to the backyard shed from the top drawer of her father's desk, she peeked through the dining room blinds once again.

The street was empty.

Locking the front door behind her, she hurried out of the house and ducked into the shed. She headed straight for the back wall and grabbed the bike she seldom rode anymore and wheeled it out.

Back inside, she found the two plastic cans of gas reserved for the snow blower stashed in the corner, exactly where they'd been when she'd checked the day before. Careful not to drip, she poured some of the gas into the detergent bottle.

With that and a hammer borrowed from her dad's toolbox stashed in her backpack, Joanna jumped onto her bike, and sticking to the rarely-used back roads, made her way to the school.

In the parking lot, she spotted the Chandlers' car immediately. It was the only red convertible, and it was the only car in the last row, the one next to the narrow strip of trees that passed for a woods. Probably their idea of protecting their precious Porsche from the other cars parked closer to the school. But it was also away from the lights.

Nice of them to make it so easy.

Joanna propped her bike against the nearest tree and pulled the hammer from her backpack. Holding it with both hands, she positioned herself close to the edge of the windshield. She stepped back with her right leg, raised the hammer above her head, and using the full strength of her yoga-toned arms, slammed it against the windshield.

A loud dull bang and...nothing. The windshield remained. Unbroken and in place.

Stepping back and raising the hammer, she tried again. And still, the windshield refused to shatter.

Her body went rigid, and her stomach lurched. She held onto the hammer with a shaking hand.

"I need to think," she whispered into the still evening air.

She swallowed, inhaled a deep breath, and blew it out through trembling lips. Slowly, she walked around the front of the car and inched her way along its side.

She tried the door handle. Locked.

She peered through the side window. Red leather seats. Nothing to help her.

A wave of nausea shot through her, and she forced herself to place one unsteady foot in front of the other and continue her path along the length of the car. With a slight pivot, she turned to face its back...and the rear window.

The *plastic* rear window.

"Yes," she hissed, blinking back the sudden tears that sprang to her eyes.

Lifting the hammer above the window, she slammed the claw end into the plastic and pulled downward in a single sharp stroke.

Rrrrrippp.

Joanna laughed out loud. Working quickly, she used the hammer and her hands to widen the tear and peel back the edges of the plastic until the former window was transformed into a large gaping hole.

She grabbed the detergent bottle, reached into the

opening, and emptied it into the car. Stepping back, she pulled the newspaper from her backpack, rolled it into a tube, and lit its end. Then, with a powerful overhand throw, she hurled it through the window. And she watched.

A flash of light.

A loud whoosh.

An orange-red flame.

A cloud of smoke.

It all happened so quickly, and it was actually kind of beautiful. But Joanna forced herself to turn away. Snatching up her backpack and the empty detergent bottle, she hopped onto her bike and pedaled home, her feet pumping up and down at breakneck speed.

She returned her bike and the hammer to their original positions in the shed, locked the door, and hurried back into the house. She rinsed out the detergent bottle and buried it deep within the hodgepodge of cans and jars that were already packed into the recycling bucket. As she wiped her hands on a towel, she spotted the insistent red blinking of the message light on the base of the kitchen phone. She pressed 'play', and Grace-ma's voice called out.

"Joanna, are you there?" A pause followed the frantic question. "Joanna, it's Grace-ma. I'm still at the school. There was some kind of incident in the parking lot. They won't tell us what it is, but they're not letting us leave. I'm not sure what's going on, but I'll let you know when I find out more. Joanna?" Another pause, and then, "I'll try your cell."

Joanna pulled her cell phone out of her backpack and listened to a similar message. She called her grandmother back from the landline.

"Joanna, where were you? Are you home?"

"Yeah, I'm home. I was in the shower when you called. I just got your messages. What happened?"

"No one knew at first. They didn't tell us right away, but there was a car fire. People are saying it was the Chandlers'."

Joanna let out a practiced gasp of surprise. "You're kidding! Was anyone hurt? Are *you* okay?"

"I'm okay, and no one was hurt, thank goodness. It happened while we were still in the auditorium. We hadn't even gone to your homerooms yet when they announced that there was some sort of 'incident', but no one was hurt. Then they said we needed to go to the gym. The teachers and the principal were there to make sure no one left."

"So, how did you find out it was a car fire?"

"They announced it later. They said the firemen were able to put it out, and only one car was damaged, and the owners had already been notified. But they think it's arson. Now the police are here, and they're meeting with each of us individually."

"So, who do they think--?"

"I don't know. I don't think anyone knows. There are all sorts of rumors flying around, but I don't know what's true. Anyway, I just wanted to let you know what's going on here. I'll be home when I can, okay?"

"Okay," Joanna said softly. "Drive safely. I love you, Grace-ma."

"I love you too, Joanna. I'll see you when I get home."

Poor Grace-ma. Her voice...so sad, so worried. It didn't even sound like hers. She was shaken up, and she was there all alone. In an unfamiliar place with people she didn't know. Joanna hadn't wanted to put her in that situation, but it was the perfect night. She'd *had* to do it then.

Her grandmother must have suspected Quinn. It was obvious. Joanna wondered if anyone else did. Yet.

I was in the shower when you called. The lie had tripped off her tongue, but it wasn't a bad idea. She sniffed her sweatshirted arm, her hands, a handful of her hair. Was there a slight smell, the faint odor of gasoline? She sniffed again. Still not sure.

Well, better safe...

The parking lot and the school building had been inspected and deemed secure, and the Back-to-School Night attendees had been herded into the gym. Grace took a lower bleacher seat next to a pair of anxious-looking parents wearing worried looks. Others huddled together in whispering clusters scattered across the shiny floor. A few loud parental complaints about being forced to wait rose above the hum of the more subdued voices buzzing through the room.

A perspiring man in a wrinkled shirt called out names in groups of ten, and people made their way to the exit door where Mr. Osborne, the principal, spoke to each of them, one by one.

"Gary and Karen Lawrence, Linda Goldman, Ted and Wendy Blewett, Grace Raymond..."

Grace sprang off the bleacher and made her way to the exit door, taking her place behind a tall couple wearing expensive-looking leather jackets.

"Please stand behind this line until your name is called again." A curly-haired woman in a navy dress pointed to the red line marking the perimeter of the polished wood floor.

Grace watched as names were read, and people, singly or in pairs, stepped up to Mr. Osborne, answered his questions, and were cleared to leave.

"Grace Raymond," the principal called out.

Grace stepped forward. "I'm Grace Raymond."

"And are you the..." He squinted and studied her face. "The...uh...mother of one of our freshmen?"

Grace flipped her graying blonde hair over her shoulder. "No. I'm Joanna Harvey's grandmother. Her parents are away this week, so I——"

"Ah...yes...Joanna. She's one of our top freshman students." Mr. Osborne smiled, his eyes crinkling at the corners. "I'm sorry you didn't get to meet her teachers tonight, but as you can see..." Pressing his lips together, he shook his head. "Anyway, is this your signature?" He handed Grace his clipboard and pointed to her handwritten name on the evening's sign-in sheet.

She nodded. "Yes."

"Okay, good. Then, please sign again in the space to the right."

Grace slid the pen from the metal bracket at the top of the clipboard and signed her name.

Mr. Osborne took the clipboard and peered down at the two signatures. "And may I see your driver's license, please?" he asked, looking up at Grace.

She dug through her bag, pulled out her wallet, and handed her license to Mr. Osborne.

"Thank you," he said, his eyes moving from Grace's face to her license and back to her face again. He handed her license back. "Did you see anything unusual in the parking lot when you arrived this evening?"

"No." Grace shook her head. "Not at all."

"Anything unusual in the building? A conversation you might have overheard? Anything that seemed odd or suspicious?"

"No, nothing," she said., her voice lowering to a whisper. "So, what do you think——?"

"I'm sorry, but I'm not at liberty to discuss the events of the evening right now. We're still gathering information. But you're free to go, Ms. Raymond. And thank you for your patience and cooperation."

Grace returned the principal's thanks, and maneuvering herself through the crowd of still-waiting parents, made her way to the exit door.

The night air was crisp and cool, and the brightly lit parking lot was flooded with people heading to their cars. At the far end of the lot, away from the stanchion mounted lights, a fire truck, two police cars, and a group of uniformed men ringed the charred metal carcass that had recently been a car. The area was cordoned off with bright yellow tape, and a policeman waved on the backed up line of vehicles slowing down as they passed the scorched remains.

Quinn...

It must have been her. She'd done it before. But why this time? Not that it mattered. Anyway, the investigators would figure it out. And then? Who knew? That would be up to the school, the authorities, her parents. She was obviously a very troubled girl, and she needed help. Whatever happened though, she wouldn't be back at Oakdale High. And that would be a good thing. For everyone.

Grace slid her key into the ignition, switched on her headlights, and joined the line of vehicles crawling past the burnt out car as they headed toward the stop sign at the end of the parking lot.

When she pulled her car into the driveway, the outside light was on, but the house was dark. She glanced down at the dashboard clock. 10:10. It was late, but not *that* late. Grace stepped out of the car and tilted her head back, looking up to the second floor.

Joanna's room was dark.

She turned her key in the lock and entered the house, flicking on the light by the door. The alarm beeped, and she punched in the code. She hung her jacket in the hall closet and crept up the stairs. The house was quiet. She tiptoed down the hall to Joanna's room. The door was partway open, the way it usually was. Easing it further ajar, she poked her head inside.

Joanna, clad in the peace-sign decorated pajamas Grace had bought her last year, lay on her side, her body curved into a parenthesis. Her shiny dark hair spilled onto the pillow.

Grace moved the door back to the position she had found it in and walked down to the guest room that had been hers all week. She changed into her nightgown, washed her face, and brushed her teeth in the bathroom next door. Stepping into the hallway, she turned toward her room. But then, with a quick pivot, she peered into the other direction, toward Joanna's door.

Moving almost soundlessly, like a cat, she slid past her room to the hallway door that opened into the other bathroom. *Joanna's* bathroom. She turned the knob and stepped inside.

Joanna's large bath towel hung on the chrome rack in the corner. Grace touched it, and yes, it was damp. Opening the door to the shower, she reached down, her hand grazing the floor, the *wet* floor.

Her granddaughter had been home all night. She had taken a shower, and now she was asleep. And very soon, Grace would be too.

34

I t had taken Joanna a while to figure out how to do it. But once she'd come up with the plan, it hadn't been difficult at all. Quinn had laid the groundwork herself. She'd already done the deed. Joanna had just needed to replicate it. And her actions were perfectly justified. Quinn deserved anything that happened to her. She should have been punished the first time, not just shuffled off to another school. *Joanna's* school. So, in a way, Joanna had provided a service to the whole Oakdale High School community.

From her regular seat at the back of the bus, she stared out the window as Fergie turned onto Evergreen Lane. No bus ride reading for her today. Grace-ma had wanted to drive her to school this morning. *What if Quinn is on the bus? She could be dangerous. Joanna, please.* But Joanna had talked her out of it. There was no way she was going to miss this particular morning's bus ride.

Quinn might be on the bus. Or not. It would depend on how long it took the school, the cops, the detectives, or whoever to put the pieces together. The evidence was circumstantial. Still, it should be enough to get Quinn kicked out of Oakdale High. If not, Joanna would have to come up with another plan.

The bus passed the first three mailboxes on Evergreen. One, two, three. It stopped in front of the fourth.

No Quinn.

"Where is that girl?" Fergie's bark was loud enough for Joanna, even in the back seat, to hear. He tapped the horn. "You kids..." He shook his head. "Too bad. I gotta go, or the rest of you are gonna be late."

With a loud grumble, the bus moved slowly past Quinn's stop. Joanna pressed her face to the window and squinted. Way down on Quinn's driveway, she could just make out a white car marked with blue letters.

Oakdale Township Police

That's what happens when you play with fire, Joanna thought, her lips stretching into a close-mouthed smile.

35

Grace understood why Joanna hadn't let her drive her to school that morning. The bus, packed with kids, some who would know what had happened the night before and some who wouldn't, would be buzzing with chatter.

A car fire? In the school parking lot? Arson? Rumors, conjectures, questions, gossip...Joanna didn't want to miss all of that. Back in high school, Grace wouldn't have either. But she had made Joanna promise that she wouldn't talk to Quinn or even make eye contact with her.

The girls didn't like each other, but there was no reason to believe Quinn would do anything to hurt Joanna. Plus, there were other kids on the bus, and the driver too. Actually, there was a good chance Quinn wouldn't even be on the bus. Still, Grace didn't want her granddaughter anywhere near her.

Leaning forward with her elbows planted on the kitchen table, Grace spooned up the last bit of oatmeal in her bowl and gazed out the window. A brick patio dressed up with thickly cushioned outdoor furniture, a stone veneer gas grill, and a fire pit opened out onto a large backyard bordered by woods. Dawn and Tom lived in a beautiful house. They had nice neighbors and a wonderful group of friends. As did Joanna. They'd made a good life, and they were a happy, well-adjusted family. All three of them. When she thought of all the years she'd spent worrying, wondering if...Grace shook her head, dislodging the thought. Everything had worked out just fine. More than fine.

Her cell phone rang, her daughter's name lighting up the screen.

"Dawn?" Grace answered, glancing up at the clock on the microwave. Ten A.M., which meant it was seven in the morning in California. "Is everything alright?"

"Everything's fine, Mom. I just wanted to know how Back-to-School Night went."

"Um...well...isn't it early out there?"

"Yeah, but I want to hear about last night."

"Well..." Grace cleared her throat.

"Well? Tell me."

Grace's lips quivered as she exhaled. "The Chandlers' car was set on fire in the parking lot last night. It happened while everyone was still in the auditorium. So, there was no Back-to-School Night."

"What?" Dawn shrieked.

"No one was hurt," Grace said quickly.

Then, forcing herself to speak slowly and calmly, she told her daughter the complete story of the night, recounting every detail from the moment she arrived at the school until the time she returned home. Dawn listened silently without speaking, without interrupting, and without questioning. Grace talked and talked until she had told her daughter all that she knew.

"Was it Quinn?' Dawn whispered.

"I don't know, not for sure. But..." Grace paused. "I think so."

"And school wasn't canceled today?"

"No, it wasn't. Joanna's bus came right on time," Grace said. "I wanted to drive her, but she wouldn't let me. I made her promise not to speak to Quinn or even look at her. I guess she didn't want to miss--"

"It's okay, Mom. There'll be plenty of other kids on the bus. Joanna will be fine. Just call me when she gets home, okay?"

"I will," Grace promised. "Oh, and I told Joanna she could have some friends over tonight. I forgot to ask you. Is that okay? I'm sorry. I didn't mean to--"

"Of course, it's okay. You know that," Dawn said. "She didn't invite Quinn though, did she?"

"No. No. Absolutely not. In fact, Joanna was thrilled when Quinn switched lunch tables the other day. So that *relationship*, or whatever you want to call it, is over. Good timing, right?"

"Yeah, that's for sure," Dawn agreed. "Oh, and Mom, do you have snacks and soda in the house? You'll need--"

"Don't worry. I've got it covered. Just enjoy the rest of your day with Tom, and I'll call you later."

They said their good-byes, and Grace rinsed her bowl and put it in the dishwasher. She had big plans for the day-- vacuuming, laundry, and a trip to the supermarket. She'd need to pick up some chips and pretzels for Joanna's friends, and she'd bake them a batch of brownies too. Then, she'd order in pizza. *Ooh...fun!*

She wiped her hands on a towel and glanced around the kitchen. Everything was in order except for the recycling bucket. It was a jam-packed eyesore, and she needed to dump it into the big bin out in the garage. She lifted the bucket and...it smelled. Not bad, but weird. It was a familiar odor, but Grace couldn't quite put her finger on what it was.

She leaned down and inhaled. Gasoline? She breathed in again. Yes, it was definitely gasoline. And the smell was coming directly from the recycling bucket. That was strange. She didn't remember using anything that would smell like gas. One by one, she pulled out the empty bottles, cans, and jars, sniffing each of them before tossing it into the sink.

Nothing.

Until...

She reached in and hooked her finger through the plastic handle of an empty detergent bottle, the one she had finished a couple of days earlier. Odd for it to have been buried so deeply in the bucket. Lifting it to her nose, she inhaled the sickly sweet smell of–– gasoline. She rinsed the bottle and smelled it again. The odor was still there. Not quite as strong, but definitely there.

But why...?

She looked down at the bottle dangling from her hand and brought it to her nose again, and...yes, the empty detergent bottle smelled of gasoline. She flung it into the recycling bucket and stepped back, her hand flying to her chest. Her jaw tightened, and the sound of her racing heartbeat thumped in her ears.

But she needed to know for sure. With wooden legs, she trudged up the stairs to Joanna's room. Stepping inside, she opened the closet and looked down at her granddaughter's blue mesh laundry bag. With trembling fingers, she lifted it by a corner and peeked inside. A black sweatshirt that she didn't remember Joanna wearing lay on top. She pulled it out and brought it to her nose.

She breathed in once and then again. Very faint, but the smell was there.

Gasoline.

Grace stuffed the sweatshirt into the laundry bag and shoved it into Joanna's closet. She slid the door closed and like a walking zombie, placed one foot in front of the other and made her way down the stairs and into the kitchen.

She had work to do, and she needed to move.

With robotic precision, she gathered up the collection of bottles, cans, and jars from the sink and carefully returned each item to the recycling bucket. Then, she carried the whole clanking mess out to the garage and dumped it into the large bin.

Back in the kitchen, she scrubbed her hands, then slathered them with the lotion Dawn kept under the sink. She pulled a can of air freshener from the cabinet and sprayed. Sniffing the air, she inhaled deeply, breathing in the artificial fragrance that obliterated the sickening smell of gasoline.

Snatching up her cell phone from the table, she pulled out a chair and lowered her stiff body into it. Slowly, she scrolled through her list of contacts and stopped at the name of her former best friend. Touching it with a shaky finger, she brought the phone to her ear.

It rang four times and then...

"Hey, you've reached Paula. I'm not here. Leave me a message please."

The phone beeped.

Grace cleared her throat, and in a frosty voice that she barely recognized as her own, she began to speak. "What was it that you wanted, Paula? Just tell me what you need—this one last time." Then, closing her eyes, she clicked off the phone.

ACKNOWLEDGMENTS

Have you ever read a book that posed a "what if" question that invaded your thoughts, haunted your dreams, and hijacked your imagination––the sort of book that absolutely refused to release you from its grasp? For me, that book was William Landay's *Defending Jacob*, the remarkable novel that forced me to ask my own "what if" question and inspired me to write *Follow the Leader*. So, to Mr. Landay, I owe you a huge debt of gratitude!

Of course, the journey from the initial flicker of a story question to the creation of a novel is a long and complicated affair best undertaken with the help of wise and talented writing, reading, and editing buddies. My sincerest thanks to Melinda Colleton, Roger Dornbierer, Jeannie Fritzen, and Suzanne Hoos. *Follow the Leader* is a stronger book because of you all, both collectively and individually.

I'm also sincerely grateful to the members of the Carolyn Denham Book Group and the MJC Book Club. Your keen insights, comments, and questions over the many years we've spent discussing books that have made us laugh, cry, at times disagree, and (on rare occasions) even shrug have helped me grow, not only as a writer, but also as a human being.

And to my children, Jenna, Michael, and now Mike—I love you *more*!

But most of all, I thank my husband, Mitch, for his calm good nature, sense of humor, unshakable support, and constant love as we face life's challenges together—always together.

ABOUT THE AUTHOR

 Francine Garson is the author of *Things*, a work of contemporary fiction. Her flash fiction received a first place award from the National League of American Pen Women in 2010 and a second place award from WOW-Women on Writing in 2013. Her creative work has appeared in a number of print magazines and online publications. *Follow the Leader* is her second published novel. She lives in central New Jersey with her husband and a mellow orange cat. Learn more at www.francinegarson.com

 twitter.com/@francinegarson

instagram.com/@francinegarson

Made in the USA
Middletown, DE
06 July 2022